COMMANDO

Book 3:
Operation Cannibal

Jack Badelaire

ONE

150 Miles South of Sollum, Egypt
October 23rd, 1941, 0900 Hours

Lieutenant James Lewis of the 11th Hussars stood in the turret of his Morris armoured car and peered through a pair of binoculars. About a mile to the south, he discerned the shape of a large vehicle sitting in the middle of the road, or what passed for a road in the middle of the Egyptian desert. Turning the focusing wheel of his binoculars, Lewis decided the vehicle was a transport of indeterminate make and model. This side of "The Wire" - the border between Egypt and Libya - Lewis imagined it was British, but he'd been in the desert long enough to know that vehicles often changed hands and moved across the relatively unsecured border, so the vehicle might belong to anyone.

Lewis looked down into the turret and caught the eye of his gunner. "Freddy, make sure the guns are loaded, and pass me the Thompson."

Lewis' gunner, Frederick Kent, reached down into the belly of the armoured car and picked up the Thompson submachine gun tucked into the corner of the crew compartment. He handed the weapon to Lewis, and followed it up a moment later with a satchel of 20-round magazines. Lewis hung the satchel from a hook on the inside of the car's open turret, then loaded the Thompson. Kent checked the magazine seating on the Bren and drew back the bolt, then he checked the magazine on the Boys anti-tank rifle, finally working the weapon's bolt action and chambering one of the rifle's massive .55 calibre armour-piercing cartridges.

"Both weapons ready for action, sir," Kent announced.

Lewis nodded and glanced back behind him. Sitting with their engines running, a half dozen lorries formed a supply convoy, bound for the Jerabub oasis, where the British had kept a garrison for the last seven months. Lewis' armoured car was the escort for the convoy, although considering the vehicle's thin armour and paltry weapons, he knew his presence was more for show than for any real protection. He was easily outclassed by any of the German armoured cars fielded by the Afrika Korps, and even the Italian cars were superior to his Morris. If they encountered any stiff resistance, Lewis' orders were to engage the enemy long enough for the convoy to break contact and escape, but Lewis didn't think his car's firepower was capable of slowing down, much less stopping, any enemy force strong enough to go hunting this side of The Wire.

Unfortunately for Lewis, just such a force had been encountered in this area several times in the last few months. Patrols and supply convoys had been attacked, either through ambush or in long-range firefights, by a force of Italian armoured cars prowling the deep desert like marauding pirates seeking to plunder heavily-laden merchant ships. Considering the cargo of food, fuel, medical supplies, and other consumables loaded into the Bedfords trailing behind him, Lewis knew his convoy would be a real prize for that Italian patrol.

Lewis glanced over at the turret's weapons. The Bren gun was all fine and dandy in the hands of the poor bloody infantry, much better than trying to drag around a water-cooled, belt-fed machine gun, but it made a poor weapon on an armoured vehicle. Likewise, the Boys rifle was, well...it was better than nothing if you were a footslogger in the mud trying to knock out a Jerry armoured car from the flank, but compared to an enemy car's 20-millimetre autocannon, it was a child's pea-shooter. The Boys was cumbersome, its bolt action was slow, and at the distances found here in the North African desert, Lewis' car would be torn apart like a tin can blasted with a fowling piece long before he got close enough for the Boys' armour-piercing rounds to have any effect.

The object of his scrutiny at that moment, however, was not an armoured car, German or Italian. Within a thousand yards, the Boys would be more than capable of penetrating the body of a lorry, and within seven hundred, the Bren would be similarly lethal. Lewis brought up his binoculars for another few seconds, and fine-tuning the focus a bit more, he thought he saw at least one man-sized figure moving near the vehicle.

He made a decision. Climbing out of the Morris' open turret, Lewis walked back to the first vehicle in the convoy and approached the driver's window. The man behind the wheel, a red-faced fellow with a kerchief wrapped around his nose and mouth to block out the worst of the dust, looked down at him.

"Well, what is it, sir?" he asked.

"There's a vehicle in the road, about a mile ahead. We'll approach within seven hundred yards, and then we'll move forward and make contact. You've got field glasses?" he asked the driver.

The man bent out of sight for a moment, then came up again holding a leather case.

"All right, keep an eye on me when we approach," Lewis continued. "If I think there's no trouble, I'll give you the signal flag left to right three times. If I want you to leg it, I'll only give you the flag left to right once. Pull back two

4

miles and wait ten minutes. If you don't see me approaching with flag in hand, make for Fort Maddalena. Understood?"

The driver nodded. "Yes, Lieutenant."

"Alright, cheers then," Lewis replied, then walked back to his car.

Lewis climbed back into the car's turret, then thumped the body of the car with his hand three times.

"Forward nice and easy, let's stop about seven hundred yards away, let the hens sort themselves out, and then we'll advance to one hundred yards," Lewis hollered down into the car's interior.

Lewis heard the muffled reply from the driver and the Morris lurched forward, rolling easily at twenty miles an hour. Lewis turned to his gunner.

"Freddy, get on that Bren. If there's any trouble, give them a full magazine to keep their heads down, then follow it with the Boys."

Freddy nodded and hunkered down behind the light machine gun, tucking the Bren's stock into his shoulder and peering through the weapon's sights.

Lewis brought the binoculars up to his eyes again, and with the proficiency of a man who'd spent several years in the turret of an armoured car, he kept his eyes on the vehicle ahead of them, even as the car lurched and bumped along. Although they were following a well-traveled path, the definition of "road" in the Egyptian desert was, to say the least, malleable. The road was little more than a track of hard-packed sand and gravel, straight as an arrow for dozens of miles at a stretch. Lewis had made this trip to Jerabub three times already, and by now he felt he knew nearly every feature along the route, sparse though they were. As they approached the mystery vehicle, Lewis knew there was no defile or other ambush site in the vicinity. If this was a means to make his convoy stop and present themselves for a surprise attack, Lewis didn't think there was anywhere the attackers could conceal themselves.

Still, he kept the Thompson close at hand.

The Morris reached a distance of seven hundred yards, and Lewis glanced back and saw the lorries forming up behind him, spacing themselves out at a distance of twenty yards apiece to help protect them from air attack. Lewis ordered the car forward once more, leaving the rest of the convoy behind.

"Easy now, Danny," Lewis cautioned the driver. "Be ready to throw the old girl into reverse at the first whiff of trouble."

"Got me hand on her knee, Lieutenant," the driver replied.

As they drew closer, Lewis saw that the vehicle was a Bedford lorry, pointed in their direction and angled slightly off the road. The bonnet was raised, and two men were standing in front of the lorry. One of the men was looking back at them with a set of binoculars, while the other was holding a rifle over his head with both hands.

The Morris car rolled to a stop, and Lewis let his binoculars hang around his neck while he cupped his hands to his mouth.

"Hello there! Lewis, Eleventh Hussars!" he shouted.

The man with the binoculars took a few steps forward and cupped his own mouth. "Stinson, Royal Army Service Corps, glad you chaps dropped by! Spot of trouble under the bonnet!"

Lewis let out a breath he didn't realize he was holding. Reaching down, he gave his gunner a pat on the shoulder.

"Keep them covered, but ease off the trigger, Freddy. Don't want to ruin the fellow's uniform," Lewis advised.

Lewis tapped on the roof of the car, and his driver rolled forward slowly, the loudest sound the tyres crunching over sand and gravel. The man who'd hailed them took a few more steps forward, his hands clearly visible away from his sides. When the Morris was only ten yards away, the man raised his hand and gave them a casual salute. The fellow was dressed in the standard British desert uniform, with a wet kerchief tied across his forehead and a corporal's insignia on his shoulder. Tall and lanky, with a strong, wiry build, and well-tanned from months in the desert, Lewis guessed the man to be somewhere in his late twenties. His sandy brown hair was bleached by the desert sun, and his handsome, friendly face was split at the moment by a toothsome grin.

"Bloody glad to see you chaps! It was getting a bit lonely out here," Stinson said.

Lewis took a closer look at the Bedford. The lorry had a canvas-covered cargo bed, and he saw daylight streaming through a handful of holes in the raised bonnet. There were also several bullet holes in the windscreen.

"I say, Corporal, were you strafed?" Lewis asked.

Stinson shook his head. "That's from a few weeks ago. Never got around to patching up the old sow. Turned out a bit of bullet frag damaged the radiator. Finally gave way, it seems, and we bled out on the way from Jerabub."

"That's quite a bit of bad luck," Lewis agreed. "A good thing we found you instead of Jerry or an Eyetie patrol over The Wire."

Stinson nodded and craned his head, looking past the Morris car and down the road. "Looks like your flock is waiting patiently, Lieutenant."

Lewis turned in his seat and looked behind him at the convoy some seven hundred yards away. He pulled up a signal flag from inside the turret and waved it left to right three times. Almost immediately he saw the lorries behind him advancing up the road.

"Can never be too careful, old bean," Lewis said. "Jerry can be a clever fellow when he puts his mind to it."

"No doubt," Stinson said. "I say, what are you carrying to Jerabub? The usual cargo?"

Lewis nodded. "No different than your run, I'm sure. Food, petrol, some medical supplies and other sundries. I say, I almost forgot! What happened to the rest of the lads who were with you? Surely they didn't leave you behind."

Stinson shrugged and looked past the Morris again towards the approaching convoy. "Archie and I figured it would be a quick patch and on we go. But whatever we try, just can't seem to keep it from pissing out like a bloke after a night at the pub."

Lewis frowned. "How long ago did they leave you? We haven't seen anyone about all day. Nothing but a clear horizon far as the eye can see."

"They were going to make for Fort Maddalena, pass along word that we're stuck out here." Stinson shrugged. "Archie and I figured we'd be taking turns between having a bit of a kip and standing watch at least until tomorrow."

"But didn't your escort have a wireless? Bloody long time to let you two sit and crisp out here," Lewis replied.

9

Stinson didn't immediately reply, instead leaning out again to look back behind Lewis' car. Lewis turned and saw the convoy roll to a halt behind him. Suddenly, a terrible thought struck him, and the hairs along the back of Lewis' neck stood on end. Moving slowly, he reached down and touched the foregrip of the Thompson next to him in the turret.

"I wouldn't do that if I were you, Lieutenant."

Lewis brought both his hands up to his shoulders. "Freddy..."

"Look to our flanks, Lieutenant," Lewis' gunner muttered.

Slowly, Lewis turned his head, looking left and right. As if by magic, eight men pointing rifles and machine pistols had appeared out of the desert sand, hunkered down in one-man foxholes. Each of the men had their weapons trained on the armoured car or one of the lorries in the convoy. Lewis saw they'd covered themselves over with sand-colored canvases, and Stinson had no doubt completed their camouflage.

Lewis slowly turned around in the turret and saw Stinson standing to the side of the Morris car, a Walther automatic in his hand pointed directly at Lewis' face. Archie stood behind the Bedford's engine block, rifle raised, his elbows resting on the body, the weapon's muzzle also covering Lewis. In the back of the Bedford, a corner of canvas near the cab had been pulled away. Inside, Lewis saw the muzzle of an MG-34 machine gun, and the deadly serious faces of the weapon's gunner and loader.

"Bloody hell," Lewis cursed.

Stinson pointed towards a foxhole to his left. "Take note of the plunger just visible above the lip of that man's fighting position, Lieutenant."

Lewis looked and saw that one of the men held his machine pistol one-handed, the magazine resting on the lip of his foxhole, while the other hand rested on the handle of what Lewis recognized to be some kind of detonator.

"We've planted a dozen five-kilogram charges underneath the road bed, going back a hundred metres. One wrong move, and I'm sure at least a few of those charges will be close enough to annihilate a fair portion of your convoy," Stinson explained.

"You rotten Jerry bastard," Lewis fumed.

Stinson shook his head. "I could have killed you and most of the men in the convoy within seconds, Lieutenant. But I abhor the unnecessary loss of life, and so I'm offering you the chance to surrender yourselves."

Lewis glanced down at his gunner, who still crouched at his position, Bren at the ready. Lewis saw lines of sweat

11

running down Freddy's face, but the man's hands were steady.

"Well, Freddy?" Lewis asked.

"Sir, you drop into the turret, and we'll give 'em a fight, sure enough," Freddy answered.

Lewis nodded. "But then we condemn the poor bastards in the lorries to a messy end. Our job's to keep those lads alive, Frederick, not get them killed."

"I'm with you, Lieutenant, no matter what," his gunner replied.

Lewis sighed, and moving slowly, he climbed out of the Morris' turret and down onto the roadbed. Stinson lowered his pistol, but kept the muzzle pointed in Lewis' general direction. With his off-hand, Lewis unbuttoned the flap of his holster and, with deliberate slowness, drew his Enfield revolver, offering it to his captor butt-first.

"All right, Stinson. You win."

Stinson nodded and took the proffered revolver, tucking it into his waistband. He then extended his open hand and offered it to Lewis, who shook it after a moment's hesitation.

"As you may have surmised, my name isn't Stinson," the German said. "I am *Hauptmann* Karl Steiner, of the *Wehrmacht* Regiment Brandenburg."

TWO

Corporal Thomas Lynch of His Majesty's 3 Commando leapt over the low rock wall, one hand braced against the ancient stones, the other clutching the pistol grip of his Thompson submachine gun. He landed with a grunt and kept running, both hands on his weapon now, holding the Thompson's ten-pound weight close to his body and keeping it from throwing off the rhythm of his stride.

Lynch's breath steamed in the cool morning air, trailing behind him as he ran as hard as his legs could carry him, hunched forward under the weight of his pack and other gear. In his two large ammunition pouches Lynch carried a dozen twenty-round magazines for the Thompson, with a pair of Mills bombs clipped to the webbing at his shoulders. Around his waist, the web belt bore a holstered .45 calibre automatic hanging at his right hip, while a pair of spare magazines and Lynch's Fairbairn-Sykes commando knife hung at his left. In his pack, Lynch carried his gas cape, rations, canteen, two magazines for the squad's Bren light machine gun, six spare magazines for the Thompson, a hundred feet of climbing rope, two spare pairs of socks, an emergency survival kit, a signal torch, and two one-pound blocks of demolitions explosive.

If he'd belonged to any other squad, the magazines and explosives might be fakes - dummy practice munitions of a similar weight and feel. But Lynch's squad spent much of its time training apart from the other Commandos bivouacked at Castle Largs, and Lynch's commanding officer, Lieutenant Price, insisted his men always train with live munitions and loaded weapons. Price always told Lynch and the others "If a man trains with false equipment, he picks up bad habits. And bad habits get men killed". In the last six months, on two separate missions, Price's twelve-man squad had lost a total of seven Commandos. Lynch knew Price refused to leave another dead soldier behind in enemy-occupied territory because of a bad habit.

Up ahead, Lynch saw a sergeant pointing to Lynch's left. Off to the side of the trail, he could see five silhouette targets set up in a staggered V formation out to a distance of fifty yards. Lynch skidded to a halt, drew back the bolt of his Thompson, brought the weapon up to his shoulder, and began to fire. Each target received a four-round burst, Lynch aiming low and riding the recoil up as the slugs riddled the silhouettes from imaginary navel to throat.

Weapon empty, Lynch pulled clear the dry magazine, tossed it aside, and re-loaded the weapon with a fresh magazine before continuing along the course.

Up ahead, a water-filled ditch ten feet wide and twenty feet long greeted Lynch. He jumped in, immediately sinking up to his armpits in cold, muddy water. Keeping his weapon raised clear, Lynch sunk down until his chin was touching the surface before crouch-walking ahead, with good reason; there were strands of barbed wire stretched over the ditch only six inches above the surface. One of the barbs scraped across the butt of the Thompson, and Lynch lowered his weapon a fraction before continuing the last few feet.

Emerging from the ditch, Lynch jumped up and down a couple of times to shake some of the filthy water loose, then heeded the bellowed demands of another nearby sergeant and took off at a run. He dodged left and right, ducking around upright wooden poles driven into the ground, with sharp wooden arms jutting out at random angles just waiting for some careless unfortunate to run into one and knock the wind out of himself. Passing the last post, Lynch turned to his left again and ran up to the first of several free-standing wooden doorways. Bracing his weapon against a doorway, Lynch locked back the Thompson's bolt, clicked the fire selector to semi-automatic, and squeezed off aimed single shots out to a hundred yards, engaging more man-sized silhouettes.

Firing his weapon dry again, Lynch performed the same reload, then continued on down the course. He approached a boulder path, jumping and weaving between the rocks at his best possible speed. At the gesture from another one of the course's watchful NCOs, Lynch tore a grenade from his shoulder, armed it, and heaved it to the side of the course as far as he could throw it, then ducked down behind a nearby boulder. A moment later he heard the flat crack of the grenade's explosion, and jumping to his feet, Lynch sprinted for the last segment of the course.

Ahead of him there were dummies in tattered field-grey, stuffed with straw. Lynch charged one and nearly tore its head clean off with a buttstroke from his Thompson. Passing the "dead" dummy, Lynch slung his submachine gun and drew his .45 calibre automatic. Racking the slide while still on the move, Lynch skidded to a stop and fired three shots at the left-hand dummy, three shots at the right-hand dummy, and a final shot back at the left. Lynch dropped the empty magazine, let the slide snap forward, reloaded his pistol, and holstered it before charging towards the final dummy. When he was no more than five feet away, Lynch drew his knife and lashed out, slashing and stabbing at the dummy's groin, stomach, heart, and throat. After the final slash, Lynch sheathed his blade and stood at attention as a whistle sounded, signaling the end of his run.

A nearby instructor looked at the stopwatch in his hand. "Final time three minutes, forty-seven seconds."

Lynch nodded, breathing hard. Six seconds faster than yesterday's run. He turned right and walked off the course, unslinging his Thompson. Keeping the weapon pointing in a safe direction, he unloaded and cleared the submachine gun before doing the same with the pistol at his belt. They took enough risks running live-fire exercises; there was no need to risk an accidental discharge off the course.

Lynch saw there was a small crowd near the end of the obstacle course. Several junior Commando officers, as well as more senior men such as Major Jack Churchill, stood in attendance along with a handful of American Marines. The Marines were commanded by Lieutenant James Tracy, a sharp, no-nonsense fellow with a keen interest in studying Commando combat doctrine and operational methods. He and his men had been living and training with the Commandos for some months. The Marines were all solid men, disciplined and enthusiastic, and every one of them was a crack shot. One of their senior NCOs, a Sergeant Edwards, had handily trumped most of the Commandos on the rifle range, his marksmanship on par with the scores of Corporal Bowen, one of the best sharpshooters in 3

17

Commando. Lynch saw the Marine sergeant in attendance; a tall, grizzled, broad-shouldered statue of a man standing at a regulation-perfect parade rest, the very image of what Lynch would describe if someone asked him what an American Marine Sergeant looked like. He'd spoken to Edwards a few times in the last couple of months, and the grey-haired veteran had been the consummate professional soldier. *Perhaps the Yanks will finally get off their arses and take up arms against old Adolf*, he mused. *Don't they know there's a bloody war on?*

"Oi, let's hear it, Tommy!"

Lynch turned to see Corporal Harry Nelson, one of his squadmates, walking towards him. Nelson had run the course earlier, as evidenced by the wet muck still clinging to his boots and battledress.

"Three and forty-seven. Yourself?"

Nelson's face screwed up in a grimace and he gave Lynch a playful punch in the arm. "Bastard! I was three seconds slower. Must be your Irish blood - makes you run faster than us honest Englishmen."

Lynch let out a guffaw. "Honest! That's a laugh, so it is. I've never met a more dishonest Englishman than you, Harry. There be dead men rotting in prison graveyards who're more saintly."

18

"More saintly, but clearly slower," Nelson replied with a grin.

The two men turned and walked back towards their barracks. When they'd first met, Lynch had been somewhat distrustful of the roguish Englishman, and with good reason; Nelson was clearly a man who'd chosen the army over an inevitable date with the hangman's noose. But although his activities before the war were no doubt less than honest, Harry Nelson was a man Lynch knew he could trust completely under the direst of circumstances. As part of the British Expeditionary Force, both had seen squadmates die a year and a half ago during the battle for France. In fact, it was the drive to strike back at the Germans as soon as possible, whatever the personal risk, which brought both men together in Colonel Durnford-Slater's elite 3 Commando. They'd fought side by side first in the small French town of Merlimont, and then again three months ago in the city of Calais. When Lynch and Price had been captured by the SS while trying to escape the city, Nelson had been one of the few who'd readily agreed with Sergeant McTeague to go back into Calais and rescue them, no matter the cost.

Nelson's willingness to dive head-first through the gates of Hell was one of the reasons Lynch was alive today, and he knew he'd do the same for Nelson in a heartbeat.

They were brothers-in-arms, and there were few bonds stronger than that.

The walk back to their squad's barracks took them past some of the other training grounds, crowded with men performing their mid-morning exercises, as well as the formidable Castle Largs itself. The morning was cold and grey with a thick cloud cover overhead and the promise of rain later in the afternoon. Fall in Scotland was a cold, wet affair, and the men of 3 Commando were working hard in anticipation of a rumored operation sometime in the next few months, possibly before the end of the year. Price hadn't mentioned whether or not his squad was going to be involved; theirs was considered an independent unit, operating partially outside of 3 Commando's normal command structure. The particulars of that arrangement were clearly beyond Lynch's pay grade, so to speak, but he was sure they had something to do with the mysterious Lord Pembroke, the elderly statesman who'd been behind the last two missions Price's squad had undertaken. Although Pembroke's degree of authority was unclear, he'd mentioned being old friends with the PM. No doubt, a word in Churchill's ear from Pembroke was enough to grant him the power to send Lynch into battle again at a moment's notice.

Nelson and Lynch entered their barracks, a smaller outbuilding set aside for their squad because of its independent status. There was some grumbling about this from other men of 3 Commando, but the decision was made in light of operational security. The other members of the troop weren't involved with their missions and weren't cleared for the details of what took place, although there were enough rumors and speculation, especially with the casualties Price's squad had taken during each of their two missions.

Inside the barracks, eleven cots lined two long walls, each with a canvas camp chair and a large foot locker. Price was bivouacked with the other officers in a separate barracks, although he did spend considerable time with his men. Several of the other squad members were sitting around the barracks space, changing out of wet uniforms, cleaning their weapons, or enjoying a breakfast of biscuits and marmalade. Corporal Rhys Bowen, the squad's sniper, was meticulously cleaning the scope of his rifle, removing the last traces of muddy water and fussing over the weapon like an overprotective parent. His spotter, the ginger-haired and gregarious Johnson, was oiling the action of his Colt .45 automatic while a cigarette dangled from the corner of his mouth.

Over in another corner of the room, Sergeant McTeague, the squad's bearlike senior NCO, leaned back in his camp chair, Tam O'Shanter pushed back on his head, and smoked a pipe while reading from a leather-bound book. Lynch recognized it as something by Kipling, no doubt some gripping tale of adventure in the exotic East. While not much of a reader himself, Lynch was even more surprised that McTeague found relaxation and enjoyment between the pages of a good book. The broad-shouldered Scotsman was a man of many surprises.

An iron stove occupied one corner of the large room, with a stack of firewood and a wooden camp table nearby. Some rickety wooden shelves contained boxes of military rations, tins of tea, and cans of sweet milk, a critical component in any good cup of char. As was to be expected on a cold morning after several hours of field exercises, Hall, the squad's medic, was tending to the stove, with a brew-up almost ready. Lynch and Nelson hustled to their bunks to grab their mess tins.

"Splashing around in all that bloody frigid water, you two need to get something hot in you before you catch a chill," Hall declared as the two hurried past him.

"Aye mother, I'll fetch my tin and be there in a moment," Lynch replied. He dropped his weapons and kit on the top of his locker, then fished around underneath his bunk, retrieving his tin cup.

Nelson saw him do this and frowned while digging through his wet, filthy pack. "Damn you, Tommy! You're supposed to pack your mess kit with the rest of your equipment." Nelson fumbled around in his pack for a moment, pulling free a cup half-filled with muck and dirty water, which he unceremoniously poured onto the floor with a curse.

"That, Harry me boy, is why I didn't follow such orders," Lynch replied with a grin, slapping the Englishman on the back as he passed him by.

"Not fair, Tommy!" Nelson growled. "Not bloody fair at all!"

"No man in this unit is here because they like to play fair, Corporal. You least of all."

Everyone in the barracks stood and saluted the trim, well-dressed figure standing in the doorway. His fitted uniform looking as fresh as the day it came from the tailor's, Lieutenant David Price appeared every inch the gentleman English officer: dashingly handsome, with blue eyes and blond hair kept neatly trimmed, a tidy moustache attempting to add an air of authority to an officer no older than the men he led into combat.

But Price was no foppish dandy, serving the Crown in the army as little more than a stepping stone to higher office. His family had a long tradition of military service, with several of his older relatives holding command positions in the Royal Navy. Price was a fighting officer, a man who took his duties to heart with a deadly conviction. Lynch had seen Price kill with automatic weapons, grenades, pistols, and even in hand-to-hand combat. Gentleman or no, Price was first and foremost a soldier.

Price returned the salutes and waved his hand towards Hall and the stove. "Drink up lads, get some char in you, it's been a cold morning. Especially you two, Tommy and Harry."

The Commandos lined up and Hall poured everyone a generous serving of hot tea dosed with a large splash of sweetened milk. Hall offered to pour Price a mug, but the lieutenant politely declined. Price waited until everyone had a chance to enjoy a few sips before he cleared his throat and addressed the men.

"Lads, your exercises and training for the rest of the day have been cancelled. Clean your kits, pack your bags, and be ready to depart by thirteen hundred hours."

"Back across the channel again is it, Lieutenant?" Nelson asked.

"No, Harry. Given the cold weather we've been having, someone in authority decided to be kind." Price gave them all a broad grin. "You're being sent somewhere with lots of bright sunshine, blue skies, and plenty of white sand."

"Oh, bloody hell," Lynch declared. "We're off to North Africa!"

Suddenly, the cold and the muck didn't seem so bad after all.

THREE

50 Miles Northwest of the Jerabub Oasis
October 23rd, 1500 Hours

Lieutenant Lewis stood in the turret of his armoured car, his arm resting against the edge of the cupola, and stared out across the Libyan desert. There was little to differentiate it from the Egyptian side of The Wire; a rock-and-sand wasteland of flat ground seared to the boiling point by the relentless, white-hot sun overhead. The wide expanse of nothing was broken up by low sand dunes or rocky hills, with bits of tenacious scrub brush clinging to life despite the desert's hostile conditions.

Lewis had imagined his first deep intrusion into Libya would be at the head of the 11th Hussars, escorting a troop of cruiser tanks as they raced into enemy territory. Lewis often pictured it in his mind's eye; pennants whipping in the air as his car ran at flank speed, the sleek shapes of British armour fanned out behind him like a wake as he crossed the ocean of sand, hunting for enemy armour formations just as the sea captains of Nelson's day hunted enemy ships.

Instead, Lewis found himself in the bag. Steiner and his squad of Brandenburgers had combed over the convoy like

26

a plague of locusts, stripping men and vehicles of any and all weapons, right down to everyone's clasp knives. The armoured car's radio had been stripped out, as well as the mounted Bren MG and the Boys rifle. One man from every lorry had been loaded into the back of Steiner's Bedford, hands bound behind their backs and covered by a machine pistol, while a Brandenburger took their place, each of the driver's bellies touched by a gun muzzle. The canvas flaps across the back of the Bedford in front of Lewis were tied up, and the MG-34 was mounted on a tripod and pointed back towards the convoy, the muzzle less than fifty feet away from Lewis.

"You really must put that frown away, Lieutenant. We're almost there. Water, hot food, and shade for you and your men await."

Lewis turned and looked at Steiner, standing in the Morris' turret with him. Freddy was tied up in the back of the Bedford, nursing a couple of bruised ribs earned by loudly protesting his separation from Lewis' side. While he appreciated Freddy's loyalty, he couldn't risk the peaceful surrender offered them by Steiner. Lewis had ordered Freddy and the others to cooperate with their captors in the interest of maintaining everyone's safety. He only hoped Freddy would keep his word.

"Whatever amenities you offer, Captain," Lewis muttered, "a prison camp is still a prison camp."

Steiner shrugged. "Such are the fortunes of war, Lieutenant. If I was more bloodthirsty, you and your men would be lying dead in the hot sand, food for the desert scavengers."

"I'm still a bit surprised you didn't just riddle us with bullets and take our convoy anyway. You've got enough bodies to handle the lorries yourselves," Lewis replied.

"As I told you, Lieutenant," Steiner said, shaking his head, "I do not take lives unnecessarily. War is terrible enough without killing men who don't need to die."

"Sounds a bit pacifistic for a Jerry officer," Lewis replied.

Steiner glared at him. "Do not make the mistake of thinking I am incapable of killing when needed." Steiner gestured towards the Bedford in front of them. "This truck was not machine-gunned by an aircraft. The occupants were less inclined than you were to accept my offer of surrender."

Lewis remembered the bullet-riddled windscreen and nodded, an icy finger running down his spine.

Eventually, Lewis was able to see around the body of the Bedford, and he spotted a low hill of ragged stone in front of them, a small fort perched on its summit. The convoy continued towards the hill, and as they grew closer,

Lewis' estimation of the hill's size was considerably revised. The hill was a good sixty or seventy feet high at its peak, and several hundred yards from end to end. The hill appeared to be a rough crescent of sun-bleached stone, and they were approaching it from the concave side of the crescent, the tips ahead and to either side of them as they drove closer. The side of the hill facing them was steep, almost sheer, and comprised of bare rock devoid of any sand or vegetation, worn almost completely smooth by the desert winds.

The hilltop fortress stood on the middle of the crescent. It appeared to be two storeys tall, built of rock similar to the hill itself, no doubt quarried nearby. Lewis saw the glint from a pair of binoculars at the top of the fort, but there was no other activity or outward signs of modern civilization.

As they passed between the tips of the hill's crescent, Lewis spotted several well-camouflaged *sangars* - redoubts of stone piled in the manner one might normally use with sandbags - covered with sand-colored canvas and camouflage netting. Lewis spied the muzzles of machine guns and at least one anti-tank gun, but he guessed that from a distance, and certainly from the air, the *sangars* were all but invisible.

Lewis saw Steiner watching him out of the corner of his eye. The German smirked. "There isn't a grain of sand within several kilometres' radius that isn't regularly swept

29

by field glasses and covered by machine guns and cannons, Lieutenant."

Lewis nodded and gestured towards one of the *sangars.* "I see you're quite adept at the art of camouflage."

"Out here in the desert," Steiner replied, "when there isn't any cover to hide under, you have to make your own."

"You can't hide the fort," Lewis pointed out.

Steiner nodded, but smirked again. "That fort has been there for years in its current state, and when we arrive, I can show you the parts of it that existed from the time of the Romans. From the air, it appears to be unoccupied. Besides, your RAF ventures this far south only rarely. They're too busy keeping an eye up north, along the coast, where the big battles are being fought, and when they do fly overhead, they're looking for swarms of panzers, fuel dumps, or airfields."

Under the watchful muzzles of several machine guns, the small convoy approached the base of the hill. Lewis noticed camouflaged netting disguising the shapes of several vehicles, and although he wasn't sure, Lewis hazarded a guess that several of them were Italian Autoblinda armoured cars. As they pulled to a stop near the parked vehicles, a number of men in Italian battledress emerged from hiding, each man carrying a rifle or machine pistol.

Curiously, each Italian sported a plume of black feathers on the right-hand side of his helmet.

Steiner touched Lewis in the ribs with his Walther. "End of the road, as they say, Lieutenant. Please exit your vehicle - slowly, *bitte*."

Warily eying the armed men surrounding them, Lewis eased himself out of the Morris' turret and onto the sandy ground. He gave the body of the car a couple of soft thumps.

"Alright, lads. Out nice and slow."

The remaining two crew members climbed out and stood shading their eyes from the sudden glare of the early afternoon sun, having been bottled up inside the car since mid-morning. Lewis saw that as each of the lorries pulled to a stop, the driver was ushered out of the vehicle by his German guard. The seven men aboard Steiner's captured Bedford climbed out of the back after the machine gun team had disembarked with their weapon and its tripod. Eventually, all sixteen British soldiers were standing in the sun, most with one hand shielding their eyes, the other hand rubbing aching backs or bums.

As soon as Freddy laid eyes on Lewis, he ambled over and leaned in close. "Not much chance in making a break for it here, sir."

Lewis shook his head. "We're surrounded by machine guns, covered by at least two dozen men that we can see, and we're...well I'm not sure where we are, to be honest. Somewhere northwest of Jerabub, would be my guess, but just how far, I've not the foggiest."

"Sir, any orders for the rest of the lads, if we find ourselves separated?" Freddy asked.

"Every man is to cooperate fully with our captors," Lewis stated firmly, seeing the defiant gleam in Freddy's eye. "We're at too much of a disadvantage here for any heroics. Steiner might be a tricksome Jerry blighter, but so far he's kept his word about our fair treatment. We shan't give him any reason to go back on that agreement. Understood?"

Freddy's lips drew into a tight line for a moment, but just as quickly he nodded, straightened up, and gave Lewis a salute. "Yes, Lieutenant."

Lewis returned the salute and nodded for Freddy to carry on, as Steiner walked over to him. "Plotting your escape already?"

Lewis heard the humor in Steiner's tone. "I've made it clear that no one is to get any...clever ideas. Besides, I think it is fairly obvious that we don't really have anywhere to go," he replied.

"*Ja*, this is true. A man would likely die of thirst and exposure miles from the nearest English outpost. But, enough of such things. Come, I will show you to your new home."

Steiner and several of his Brandenburgers led Lewis and the other captives off to their left, away from the camouflaged vehicles and towards the steep slope of the hill. Lewis saw that several Italian soldiers were hammering man-high stakes into the sandy earth, while other men wound and stretched barbed wire between the stakes. Although Lewis wasn't a country lad, he was reminded of a farmer's cattle fence, perhaps something that might be seen out in the American West.

As the wire was being strung, other men were unrolling and laying out another large section of camouflage netting. With a couple of taller stakes planted in the middle of the confined area, Lewis saw that the netting would be set up as a kind of tent. Watching them work, he was struck by the speed and efficiency of the Italian troops; he'd only seen them up close as prisoners of war, or at a distance during an exchange of fire. Even so, their reputation among the British forces was less than flattering. He also noticed that the Italians ran everywhere they went, even if it was only a short distance. Perplexed, Lewis asked Steiner about the Italians' odd behavior.

"I was given my pick of the 10th Bersaglieri," Steiner replied. "An elite unit of light infantry, well-trained and highly motivated. They have been conditioned to run everywhere they go, even while carrying out mundane tasks.

The black feathers they wear are the sign of their unit. A little conspicuous on the uniform of a modern soldier, but they are quite a sight."

Lewis' estimation of Steiner rose several notches. If a mere captain could pick and choose from the elite units of an ally's army, just what kind of authority did he possess?

Soon, the Italians were finished, and the British were ushered inside the fence. Lewis was held back from entering with the rest by a touch on his arm from Steiner.

"You will eventually be confined with the rest of your men, Lieutenant. However, as one officer to another, I would like to share a meal with you up in the fort."

Lewis saw Freddy and the others looking at him from underneath the dappled shade of the camouflaged netting as the Italians secured the last few strands of wire. The men were unsure of just what his separation from them meant.

"I won't eat unless I know my men will be taken care of at the same time," he replied.

Steiner nodded. "Of course. We shall give them water now, but then they will be given tools and ordered to dig a latrine pit in the corner of their confinement. Once that is done, they will be provided a meal. From now on, you will be fed twice daily, morning and evening, and an extra half-ration of water given in the middle of the day."

Lewis grunted his acceptance of Steiner's terms. Given the sparse rationing of food and water that combat troops lived with in the desert, Steiner was being considerably generous with his provisions, especially the water.

"You must have quite the cistern, to be able to water us like we're houseplants, Captain," Lewis said.

Steiner grinned, and motioned for Lewis to follow him. "Come, let me show you the font from which my generosity flows."

They walked back towards the center of the hill's crescent, this time walking behind and underneath the camouflage netting that covered Steiner's motor pool. As Lewis had guessed, the netting concealed a half-dozen Autoblinda armoured cars, each painted in desert tones, all appearing well-maintained and ready to depart at a moment's notice. There was also a Kübelwagen and a German Opel Blitz, both bearing the palm tree and swastika of Rommel's Afrika Korps.

Soon they passed by the vehicles and came to a stop at a circular well of stacked stone, covered by a wooden lid. A hand pump was driven into the ground next to the well, with a curled length of rubber hose attached to the pump. Steiner lifted the lid and gestured for Lewis to look inside. The well was dark and the angle of the sun was such that he didn't see anything, but Steiner dropped a small pebble into the well, and after a moment Lewis heard the distinct splash of the pebble entering deep water.

"An underground spring flows below us," Steiner explained. "We think it is one of the waterways that feeds the Jerabub oasis, far to the southeast. I don't think they miss what we take away for our own purposes."

"Bloody brilliant," Lewis murmured. "You've got your own water supply. No wonder you can sit out here in the desert with so many men."

Steiner nodded. "We need other consumables, of course, but it is much easier to bring food and fuel, rather than water, this far into the desert."

"I suppose this well was here before you arrived?" Lewis asked.

"*Ja*, it might date back to when the Romans built the fort; a crack in the stone here might have brought some trickle of water to the surface. The well had collapsed when the Italians found it years ago, but they dug it clear and rebuilt it."

As Steiner spoke, one of his Italians ran up to them, and with a nod to Steiner, picked up the end of the hose and dropped it into the well, the length flowing through his fingers until Lewis heard the end hit the water. The Italian then positioned a water can under the mouth of the pump and started to work the handle. After a minute of hard labor, clear, bright water began to pour from the pump's nozzle, and soon the water can was full. Another Italian approached at a run and took that can away, while a third jogged over carrying two other cans.

"Come," Steiner told Lewis, "let us make our way up to the fort."

The two walked away, in the opposite direction from where his men were kept, and eventually they approached a set of iron rungs hammered directly into the rock of the hill. The rungs had been painted a light khaki color to help them blend in. Steiner began to climb, and Lewis followed, quickly discovering that even with their light-colored paint job, the iron rungs were scorchingly hot to the touch. Several times Lewis felt himself teetering on just his toes as he played a kind of "hot potato" with the ladder, shifting his hold from one hand to the other every few seconds to keep from burning his palms.

Eventually they made it to the ridgeline, Steiner offering Lewis a steadying hand at the top of the ladder. Turning and looking back, Lewis was stunned for a moment by the spectacular view across the desert. From fifty feet up, the horizon pushed back a few miles, and the sheer enormity of the desert became even more evident.

"Quite the view from up here," Lewis said.

Steiner chuckled. "At first, it just appears to be more of nothing, yes? But after a while, you begin to appreciate the epic scale of the desert. It is an ocean of sand and rock, a whole new world for Europeans such as ourselves, men used to forests and green grass."

The two men began to make their way along a rough path to the fort. From this vantage point, signs of modern inhabitants were more obvious; *sangars* with mortars and 20mm anti-aircraft cannons were hidden by more netting, and each emplacement contained one or two men with field glasses, constantly scanning some quadrant of the desert or the sky above.

"That must be quite the monotonous task," Lewis remarked.

"It is, but of course, our lives depend on constant vigilance. The men know dereliction of duty here comes with a death sentence."

"Is there ever anything to see?" Lewis asked.

"Desert people wandering past, from time to time. Some of them know we are here, but they leave us alone. I offer an extra water ration or other luxuries to the first man on watch who spots movement, so it becomes a challenge to the men."

Steiner led Lewis into the fortress, the doorway guarded by an Italian sentry with a Beretta machine pistol across his chest. The sentry's serious mien coupled with his black-feathered helmet seemed to Lewis a bit ridiculous, but the soldier's bearing and demeanor suggested that he best keep his opinions to himself.

Once inside the courtyard, Lewis saw that almost every piece of equipment, every supply crate or container, every weapon or other item was either covered by some kind of camouflage, or had a cover nearby, ready to be used. Lewis guessed that once an air alert was given, everything was covered or moved inside and out of sight.

They disappeared into one of the fort's rooms off the courtyard, a large, narrow hall that served as the mess. Lewis and Steiner sat at a wooden table on folding stools and were served by one of the Italians. Tin mess plates of biscuits, marmalade, cheese, and bully beef were served, as well as tin cups of water, kept relatively cool by the well. Lewis chuckled in spite of himself at the fact that they ate British rations captured from his own convoy.

"Is everything to your liking?" Steiner asked, without a hint of insincerity.

"Other than the fact that my captors are serving me the very supplies I was supposed to protect, everything is just fine. Forgive me for finding my situation somewhat embarrassing."

"Ah, yes," Steiner replied. "It is rather insensitive, but necessary. Your supplies will provide us with food for several weeks, and much-needed fuel for our vehicles and our generator. I thank you again for cooperating, and not putting us in a position where we had to not only end your lives, but destroy your convoy as well."

A thought occurred to Lewis. "Your English is quite good, Captain. May I ask where you studied?"

"My father is a businessman, working for Siemens." Steiner replied. "Before the war, my family lived in England for five years, and I went to school there, in London. When the *Heer* began to mobilize, those of us who spoke English well were recruited and asked to serve in special units. So, here I am."

Lewis wondered how a wealthy German who studied in England and spoke the language of his enemies fluently found himself stationed in North Africa, out in the middle of the desert, with only a handful of other Germans and some Italians to keep him company. Was this a punishment of some kind, or was the chance to put Lewis and his lads in the bag worth Steiner's talents?

Steiner wiped a biscuit crumb from the corner of his mouth and smiled. "I suppose it is my good fortune to have taken you prisoner, because now I have a conversation partner who appreciates stories from my days living in your country."

"Good fortune, indeed..." Lewis muttered, eyeing his last biscuit.

FOUR

Over Mersa Matruh, Egypt
October 28th, 0400 Hours

Lynch peered out of the front cockpit windows of the modified Halifax bomber, looking down at the Egyptian coastline. Only a thin line of phosphorescence from the surf gave any clue they were approaching land; every man-made structure below was dark with strict blackout discipline. The nose of the bomber was pointed down fifteen degrees, and Lynch's hands were white-knuckled as he held onto the doorframe leading into the cockpit.

"You daft wanker, what're you doing out of your seat?" the co-pilot shouted at Lynch when he was noticed. "Go back and sit down, we'll be on land in a few minutes, provided we don't hit the water at several hundred knots!"

The aircrew laughed, as if the co-pilot's comment about crashing was the height of comedy. Lynch managed to turn himself around, still clutching at the airframe, and walked back to his spot on the makeshift canvas bucket seating bolted to the aircraft's fuselage. Lynch made eye contact with Lieutenant Price, who just shook his head.

"I told you they wouldn't want you nosing about the cockpit, Corporal," Price said.

"Just needed to see outside this big cigar sleeve, sir," Lynch muttered, sitting down.

This was the first long flight Lynch had ever taken. He'd been on short hops before, but they'd all been over English soil, in fair weather and with little danger of German air attack, poor weather, or zero visibility. Over the last two nights, however, the Halifax had carried them low over the water and without running lights in the dead of night, flying around Spain and Portugal to finally land on Gibraltar. For the sake of operational security, the plane was taxied into a hangar, where they were allowed to get out and walk around, eat a hot meal, and sleep on cots during the daylight hours. However, they boarded again and flew out after dark to make the long, harrowing journey lengthwise across the Mediterranean.

A few minutes ago, the Halifax had gained some altitude, and was now in its final landing approach. Lynch felt the plane shuddering in the air, fighting to keep from stalling as its speed and altitude decreased in just the perfect proportions for a safe landing. Fighting to remain calm, Lynch clutched at the wooden frame of his seat, forcing his mind to think of the process involved in field-stripping his Thompson, anything to keep out thoughts of the Halifax hitting the water and disintegrating, every man inside either torn to pieces and battered about by the wreckage, or drowned inside the crumpled fuselage, fingers scrabbling and scratching at the sheet metal as they fought to escape, the pressure rising, forcing the water down throats opened in a final, futile scream...

Lynch stifled what would surely have been a hysterical shriek as the Halifax jolted on impact, but the lack of cold, rushing water, or a fireball rolling through the interior of the fuselage, assuaged his fears of a horrific death. Lynch opened his eyes, not realizing that he'd closed them, and saw his squadmates sitting around him, several of them looking at him and chuckling.

"Typical bloody Irishman," Nelson laughed. "You'll charge Jerries with nought but a knife in your hand, but a wee plane ride and you're near to wetting your trousers."

"Typical bloody Englishman," Lynch retorted. "Too stupid to understand that if man was meant to fly, God would have given him wings. You'd be laughing all the way to the bottom of the Med if we'd hit the water instead of the runway."

"The two of ye," Sergeant McTeague rumbled from further down the row of seats. "Why must I always tell ye to shut yer flapping gobs?"

Nelson grinned at Lynch, who returned his look with a rude gesture and a wink.

By now the Halifax had taxied off of the landing strip, and glancing forward through the cockpit, the Commandos saw were being brought inside another hangar. The engines slowed to idle, then quit one after another, and the silence after so many hours of their deafening roar was a little unsettling.

One of the Halifax's crew emerged from the cockpit and unsecured the door. With a creak of its hinges, the portal swung open, and an oval of light shined into the fuselage. Almost immediately, a wave of warm, dry air flooded the cargo compartment, causing the men to doff their stocking caps or loosen the collars of their battledress. Seconds later, a man wearing the uniform of the Eighth Army stuck his head into the Halifax.

"'Ello gents! Welcome to Egypt! Captain Nigel Abercrombie, at your service!" he said.

Abercrombie was a grinning, gabbing, back-slapping tornado of magnanimity. Within moments of his arrival, the Commandos - already sweating in the oven-like heat of the metal aircraft hangar - disembarked from the Halifax and escorted by Abercrombie to a long row of wooden tables and camp stools, a late-night meal of sandwiches, cold water, and hot, sweet tea awaiting them. The men began their attack run on the food and tea, only to be halted by a look from Price and a growl from McTeague.

"We ain't all here yet, lads," the sergeant warned.

As if on cue, a door along the side of the hangar opened.

When word had come down that their squad would be accompanied by more Commandos, there was some degree of consternation among the men. After all, they'd been hand-picked to fight together as a small unit of just twelve men - why bother fielding them on a mission with other squads? When they learned that not only were they just one of three squads, but Price wouldn't be the commanding officer on the mission, there was nearly a riot. Only a silencing roar from McTeague had kept the men in line; that is, until they learned who was leading their mission.

Captain William Eldred was a career soldier who'd served in Egypt, Singapore, India, and the battle for France. As a lieutenant in the Duke of Wellington's Own Regiment, 2nd Battalion, Eldred fell deathly ill in late 1938. He was shipped back to England to recover, then assigned a place in the ranks of the 1st Battalion only six months before they shipped out as part of the BEF.

Eldred's new battalion fought a brutal delaying action against the *Wehrmacht* during the Dunkirk evacuation. Not satisfied with simply holding the line, Eldred and his men launched several hard-fought counterattacks against the encroaching Germans, driving them back and buying time for more men to be evacuated from the bloody beaches. Eldred's command element was hit by mortar fire after one such action, and he suffered shrapnel wounds to the right side of his face and body. Torn and bleeding, but not broken, Eldred went on to lead several more assaults before his unit was finally recalled, some of the last British soldiers to leave France.

Not content with sitting out much of the war on British soil, waiting months or even years before getting back into the fight, Eldred volunteered for assignment to a Commando troop the moment he heard of their existence. Although past the age of forty, Eldred was in fine physical condition despite the injuries received defending Dunkirk, and soon he became one of 3 Commando's leading officers. When Lieutenant Price learned that Eldred was going to be assigned to head this mission, the men were amused to hear their normally reserved leader mutter to himself, "those poor bloody Jerries...".

Now, Captain Eldred entered the hangar, followed closely by two squads of Commandos led by Sergeants Donovan and Peabody. The two other squads had flown in their own Halifaxes. It had been decided that, despite Mersa Matruh no doubt containing sufficient supplies for the thirty-seven Commandos, they would bring their own arms, ammunition, and equipment in order to maintain as much operational security as possible.

Eldred strode over to Price and shook his hand. "Well, David, it appears we all made it onto the ground in one piece. I shan't say the hard part's over, but it is something of a relief."

"Not to mention being able to stretch one's legs and find a hot cup of char waiting," Price replied.

Although Eldred was not a small man, his five-foot-six frame was almost a head shorter than Price's six foot height. Built like a bulldog, Eldred sported broad shoulders and a barrel chest, with thick, muscular arms and legs. His close-cut hair was dark brown shot through with a heavy dose of grey, and the right side of his face and neck bore shrapnel scars. When he walked, if one knew to look for it, a slight limp in Eldred's gait was noticeable, but Lynch had seen first-hand that the Commando captain could hold his own on the training grounds and running the obstacle course.

Once all the Commandos had filed into the hangar, Eldred nodded to Price and the three squad sergeants. "Alright gents, it's been a long night. Tuck in."

The three dozen men descended on the tables with a speed and precision that'd make any training instructor proud. Within moments, faces now shining with sweat were bent over tin plates, hands were jostling for first helpings, and mouths were being burned by hot tea gulped far too quickly. Lynch acquired a bacon sandwich for himself, as well as a cup of tea loaded with so much sweet milk it was more white than tan. Sandwich in one hand, tea in the other, he alternated between the two, his lingering nerves from the flight and the discomfort from the heat quickly forgotten with his first several bites.

Out of the corner of his eye, Lynch could see Price, Eldred, and Abercrombie, along with the sergeants, standing off to the side, talking softly amongst themselves Price had been unusually light on the details of this mission, to the point where Lynch didn't think his commanding officer knew any more than his men. This was troubling, since on the previous two missions, not only had Price been fully briefed, he'd briefed all his men as well. In a small, high-risk unit such as theirs, it was important for every man to know as much as possible, because it was all too likely that the officers and NCOs could become casualties before providing their men with the operational details.

Within a few minutes most of the men, well-trained in the art of eating their meals as quickly as possible, had partaken of their fill of food and drink. They were now wiping crumbs from their mouths and sweat from their brows with their sleeves, while they sat back and patted their full stomachs or ground knuckles into backs still sore from the long flight. The officers and sergeants now turned from their private conversation and approached the men, gesturing for everyone to remain seated.

Eldred stepped forward, Abercrombie to one side, Price at the other. All conversation among the men was immediately silenced.

"Well, lads, I know you've all been wondering what the devil you're now doing thousands of miles from home, sitting in a hangar in the wee hours partaking of bacon sandwiches and tea. Operational details were withheld from all of us - not just yourselves - in the event we were forced down and captured while on route. Now that we're here, however, we've been given our orders.

"Some time in the next two months, the newly-formed British Eighth Army is going to launch a massive armoured assault deep into Libya. The routes to be used for this invasion are in the process of being determined, mostly through the use of some new recce units specially trained for deep desert operations. It is vital that not only are these patrols able to carry out their missions, but that they go undetected and unmolested by the other side.

"Recently, it has come to the attention of Eighth Army intelligence, of which Captain Abercrombie is a part, that the enemy is operating a raiding unit out of a hidden base somewhere far to the southwest, possibly near the Jerabub oasis, one of our southern outposts. These raiders have, on several occasions now, either destroyed or captured supply convoys bound for our more remote outposts, including Jerabub and Siwa. In addition, they have fired on and driven off several patrols sent into the area to locate their base of operations.

"Although there are elements here in Egypt that could be used for this mission, it was decided that we should be brought in from England instead. Those units that could be used are either preparing for the imminent invasion, tasked with their own pre-invasion missions, or simply possess too many operational details, making their capture too much of a liability. In effect, our greatest asset to Eighth Army is our strategic ignorance."

There were more than a few chuckles from the men over Eldred's last remark.

Eldred continued. "Sunrise will be in just a few hours, and to maintain security, you'll be confined here within the hangar until nightfall, at which time you'll depart for a rendezvous with one of these desert reconnaissance groups. They will be taking you out into the deep desert, where your mission will be to neutralize the enemy camp once the desert group sniffs them out. Captain Abercrombie?"

Abercrombie took half a step forward. "Lads, I'm a wee bit embarrassed to say this, seeing as I'm one of our intelligence officers, but this city is downright lousy with enemy informants. Not only are half the locals on the enemy's payroll, but there have been recent rumors - *only rumors*, mind you - of German spies operating as Englishmen, right here in Mersa Matruh. I'm sure by now Jerry has sussed out that we're planning something before the end of the year, a follow-up to Operation Compass, but hopefully he doesn't know when or where we plan to strike. If he learns of your presence here, and your mission, we fear that he'll be able to alert the enemy and Rommel will either withdraw, reposition, or reinforce your target before you arrive. This is why we need to keep you lads out of sight until we send you off."

With this, Abercrombie stepped back, and Eldred nodded in agreement.

"All right, any questions?" Eldred asked his men.

Nelson stood up, gave Eldred a quick salute, and tugged at the collar of his battledress with a hooked finger.

"Beggin' your pardon, Captain, but can we do anything about this bloody heat?"

FIVE

Mersa Matruh Airbase
October 28th, 2100 Hours

His first day in Egypt had been one of the most miserable experiences of Lynch's life. Sure, being shelled by the Germans during the battle for France had been terrible, and their retreat back in July through the streets of Calais had been equally awful. But on those occasions, Lynch had been fighting for his life - he'd been engaged, filled with excitement and the sensation of pushing himself to the limit in order to survive.

But sitting in that tin oven masquerading as an aircraft hangar had been nothing but purest misery, without the benefit - if one could call it that - of danger and adventure. The three dozen Commandos were issued Eighth Army battledress, their old uniforms and insignia packed away out of sight from any prying eyes. The men re-packed their gear, cleaned their weapons and double-checked their ammunition and other supplies. All of this was accomplished just as the sun's first morning rays struck the hangar and began to bake those within like a cottager's pie.

Eldred, Price, and the squad sergeants informed the men that they should sleep if possible, and drink plenty of water in order to stay well hydrated. They did the best they could, but men who were used to the cold autumn weather of Scotland were completely incapable of sleeping during the heat of the day. The men stripped off their battledress blouses, combat boots, even their shorts, lying on cots in nothing but their undershirts and undershorts. Some men, despite the protests of anyone in their vicinity, stripped off even those garments in an effort to stay cool. Fans had been set up, and their high-pitched mechanical drone filled the hangar as their blades tried to push air around in an attempt to cool the men off, but to most of them the scorching temperatures meant moving the air around did little to relieve their suffering.

Lynch lay on his cot and stared up at the corrugated metal roof, the air at the top of the hangar shimmering with the heat of the sun searing the metal like a blast furnace. He wouldn't have been surprised if the roof itself started to melt. He'd soaked a kerchief in water and tied it around his forehead in the hopes that the evaporating moisture would keep him cool, but the dry, hot air sucked the moisture from the kerchief almost as fast as he could wet it.

After several hours of fitful, sweltering slumber, the men had been fed a midday meal of biscuits and some fruit, and the sergeants made sure every man took a salt pill and drank a full canteen of water. Several men joked that in all their time in the military, those were the easiest orders they'd ever carried out. They were also let outside in small groups of three or four men at a time and directed towards the privies, since there were no such facilities in the hangar. The men had to walk outside a hundred yards in the blazing sun, and one of the Commandos from another squad declared, "How can anyone fight in this bloody heat? The desert must be the victor in every tussle."

Eventually the minutes turned to hours, and as Lynch watched through a small window in the hangar door, the sun slowly sank below the edge of the desert; one minute the sky was a bright cerulean blue, and only minutes later, the western horizon was a quickly darkening purple, while the eastern sky was already black and carpeted in stars.

"Bizarre how that happens so bloody quickly."

Lynch turned and found Nelson standing next to him, looking out the window over his shoulder.

"It's the latitude, so I've heard," Lynch replied. "Something about being closer to the equator means the sun sets faster here than back in Blighty."

"Where'd you hear that?" Nelson asked.

Lynch shrugged. "Can't rightly remember. Maybe one of me former sergeants. Some of those old codgers had been to Africa, the Far East, all over the world, so they had."

"How bloody nice for them," Nelson grunted. "I'm going to take a piss, been holding it until the sun went down."

"I'll take the walk now," Lynch replied. "Knowing how dumb you are, someone's got to tell you where to point it."

As the two men walked past Corporal Bowen, the lean Welshman sat up from his cot. "Where're the two of you headed?"

"Off to take a piss," Lynch replied. "Care to make it a party?"

Bowen stood up and slipped his knee-length shorts and boots on. Lynch noticed Bowen's belt was adorned with pistol, magazine pouches, and his Fairbairn-Sykes knife.

"We aren't going on patrol, Rhys," Lynch said, gesturing to the weapons on Bowen's belt.

"We're in the middle of a bloody war zone, you berk," Bowen replied.

Nelson rolled his eyes. "We're in the middle of a damn airbase, a hundred miles from the lines!"

Bowen shrugged. "Fine. You walk around unarmed and without a care in the world."

The wiry sniper walked off towards the hangar door. Lynch and Nelson looked at each other.

"The heat's baked his brain already!" Nelson exclaimed.

Lynch watched Bowen walk off, then stepped to his bunk, pulled his Colt automatic from its holster, checked the chamber, and slipped the pistol into his trouser pocket.

"Aye, but that doesn't mean he's wrong," Lynch replied, and followed after Bowen.

After a moment's pause, Nelson cursed under his breath, then took a moment to fetch his own pistol before hurrying after his two squad-mates.

Even though the sun had set only a short while ago, already the air was beginning to cool, and there was a welcome breeze coming from the coast to the north. The perspiration on their bodies immediately began to dry in the outside air, and all three men took a moment to savor the first pleasant experience of the day.

"Pity it wasn't like this all the time here. I'd almost enjoy it," Nelson said.

Bowen shook his head slightly. "It'll get cold tonight. If you come out here in a few hours, you'll start to shiver. We didn't notice it so much when we arrived because the hangar trapped all that heat, but this time of the year, the desert can be frigid at night, just as it can still bake you during the day."

Nelson looked back and forth between Bowen and Lynch. "Where'd you two find so much bloody time for tucking away these odds and ends about the desert? A couple regular Lawrences of Arabia, you are."

Lynch let out a quick laugh. "Now look who's showing off. Come on, let's go take our piss and be done with it."

The three men ambled across the airbase grounds towards the privies. Although it was sundown and the base was under blackout conditions, the moon was bright enough for the men to see where they were going. As they walked, they noticed other servicemen walking in one direction or another, some carrying supplies, others simply going about the business of a war that continued around the clock. Lynch supposed that if he were one of them, he'd actually prefer to do most of his assigned tasks after the sun had disappeared for the night.

The three men did their business at the privy - holding their breath throughout, as the day's sun had boiled the privy's contents into a particularly malodorous stew - and began their walk back to the hangar. As they walked, Lynch noticed one of the locals, a young Egyptian man with a sack in one hand and a long wooden stick in the other, a nail poking out at the end, impaling an empty cigarette package.

The man appeared to be wandering about jabbing and collecting refuse.

Lynch was just about to walk past, when something tickled the back of his mind, some notion that things weren't quite as they seemed. Stopping and looking at the man again, Lynch realized he'd been out collecting refuse along the same grounds earlier in the day. Nothing to be concerned about at first, but given Abercrombie's warning about spies and informants, Lynch wondered just how much rubbish could be found after half a day of patrolling the same ground over and over.

The two Commandos with him noticed Lynch had fallen behind. Bowen and Nelson turned, and the latter spoke up. "What's the matter Tommy? Leave something behind you meant to bring back?"

Lynch nodded his head towards the Egyptian. "Either of you remember seeing that fellow over the course of the day?"

Nelson shook his head, but Bowen - the most eagle-eyed member of the squad, and the most naturally observant man Lynch had ever met - narrowed his eyes in thought.

"You're right, Tommy. All day long, that bloke's been about. Can't be that much rubbish lying around the airfield..."

At that moment, the Egyptian turned and glanced in their direction. Seeing the three British soldiers standing and staring at him, the man stopped and stared back, his stick raised halfway to his bag.

The English, Lynch knew, especially those in the military, had a tendency to not pay attention to the local help. They swept floors, polished boots, washed clothes, and served at the officer's mess, and for the most part, were noticed and scrutinized with no more attention than you'd pay to a sideboard or camp stool. Which is why, he realized, no one gave a second thought to someone walking around in the dark outside of an aircraft hangar, poking at rubbish with a stick.

An aircraft hangar filled with men who've been locked up during the heat of the day, only coming out to take a piss.

Even in the moonlight from forty feet away, Lynch saw the Egyptian's eyes, sharp as an eagle and locked onto his own. The moment drew out, and ever so slowly, Lynch saw the man shift his weight, his feet sliding in the sand.

"He's gonna bloody rabbit!" Lynch shouted.

And with that, the Egyptian dropped his sack, spun around, and took off at a dead sprint. The three men glanced at each other.

"Bugger this," Nelson said finally, "after the bastard!"

They began to chase the Egyptian, and within a hundred feet all of them realized they were in trouble. The heat of the day had sapped the strength from their bodies, and they were growing winded already, while their quarry was widening the gap between them with every stride. Although the Egyptian had appeared skinny and listless, he was clearly in better condition than he looked, and he possessed the speed and agility of the fastest street urchin.

As they left the hangars behind and began to cross the airstrip, Lynch saw ahead of the Egyptian a pair of sentries walking their patrol, rifles slung over their shoulders.

"Hey, you lot!" he shouted, waving his arms to get their attention. "Stop that blighter!"

The sentries jerked to a halt and turned, seeing the Egyptian sprinting right for them. One of them put up his hand and shouted something unintelligible, while the other began to unsling his rifle. Barely breaking his stride, the Egyptian raised and threw his stick, which sailed through the air like a javelin and stabbed into the gut of the sentry raising his rifle. The man cried out and tumbled onto his backside, the rifle flying from his hands. The other sentry, realizing the situation had just turned deadly, moved to unsling his own rifle when there was a flash of silver moonlight in the Egyptian's hand and suddenly the second sentry cried out and fell, a dark stain spreading from his side. The Egyptian didn't slow down, instead simply running past the two wounded Englishmen.

"Bloody Jesus - the bugger's knifed 'em!" Nelson puffed out as they ran.

They were approaching the other side of the airbase, closer to the city itself, and without a word they all realized that their quarry was going to get away if they didn't push it. Redoubling their efforts, panting and gasping in the night air, the three Commandos sprinted as hard as they could, arms and legs pumping, boots throwing plumes of sand with every footfall. Slowly, they began to gain ground.

SIX

Mersa Matruh Airbase
October 28th, 2115 Hours

The Egyptian glanced behind him and saw his pursuers still hot on his trail, heard the rhythm of their breathing as they charged after him. The knife in his hand was wet with the blood of the sentry he'd slashed, and he felt the droplets on the back of his hand drying in the cool night air, the congealing blood causing his skin to tighten as the moisture evaporated.

Gahiji didn't know how it all went so wrong, so fast. For weeks he had done as the Germans had asked; he'd worked on the British airbase, performing menial tasks and obeying to the best of his ability. But all the while, Gahiji was also watching, and more importantly, he was listening. Born of parents who had worked for Englishmen in the past, he'd been taught how to speak the language, his mother and father understanding that with the way the world seemed to be shrinking every year, speaking English was a prized skill, one that might someday earn him a place serving British or American businessmen.

When war came to Egypt, Gahiji made a series of cautious requests to certain individuals of ill repute who found him an audience with another Egyptian, a wealthy smuggler who worked for the Germans. Once the English turned the city into an armed encampment, the Germans would pay very handsomely for any information that could be brought out of the British military bases; troop movements, supply shipments, and most important of all, any concrete information about new offensives. Any guilt Gahiji might have felt about spying on the British immediately disappeared when he realized he made more in a week informing for the Germans than he earned in a month working on the British airbase.

He had been employed by the British for three months now, and although he let on that he spoke a handful of English words, the white men around him had no idea he could decipher most of their conversations. Of course, there were some words or phrases that bewildered him, or seemed to mean something other than what he thought. And some of them were easier to understand than others; the Englishmen were easy enough, but the Australians and New Zealanders were very hard to understand, and the Scottish were almost incomprehensible.

Still, he had been proud of what small tidbits of information he was able to feed the Germans. Gahiji was smart enough to know that this was only one small corner of what would continue to be a much larger war, and it wouldn't be over anytime soon. North Africa was a vast space, an ocean of sand, and it would take the British many more months, years perhaps, before they'd be able to drive out the Germans. With the money he was saving, buried in the dirt underneath his cot, by the time the Germans could pay him no longer, he would have enough money to see his brother and sister safe through the dangerous times that were sure to come.

But first, he had to escape these three British soldiers.

Gahiji didn't understand why he'd panicked; he'd been around such men for months, and none of them had given him a second glance. He was just another skinny brown boy, doing jobs too common and menial for the whites to do themselves. But there had been something in the way the black-haired man had stared at him, an intensity to his gaze that Gahiji had felt, even at a distance and by the light of the moon. It was as if the man was weighing his soul, measuring whether he was truly as he seemed or if he was an enemy, a deceiver. None of the British had ever looked at him like that, like a lion gazing at its prey before it sprang in for the kill. Gahiji had become unnerved, had involuntarily moved as if to escape, and as soon as he'd done so the Englishman had sensed his true purpose. The only option left had been

65

to run, to try and escape from the airbase and lose himself in the city.

Desperation drove his pace as he sought to escape his pursuers. Although he had run, he might have possibly talked his way clear, pleading shaken nerves and terror at the thought of being beaten by the English for some imagined slight. But attacking the sentries - another stupid, *stupid* move on his part - had sealed his fate. An innocent man might panic and run, but only a guilty man would wound or try to kill in order to escape.

Gahiji reached the other side of the airbase and darted around a building, nearly bowling over a couple of Egyptian laborers in the process. Shouting a hurried apology over his shoulder out of habit, he tucked his chin into his chest and ran as fast as his legs could piston against the sandy earth. He decided that he had only one hope for survival; he had to seek the aid of other Egyptian spies. Masud and Hamadi lived on the base itself, sharing a hovel close by. They were both older, and had helped him get employed on the base, vouching for his trustworthiness. Now, he had to rely on them for more than a job - he had to rely on them for his life.

Glancing back behind him, he saw the British had fallen behind again, but they were still close enough that they would find him, given time. Once they lost him, they would raise the alarm, and the whole British army would descend on him. Discovery would only be a matter of time. If, however, the three men could be killed quickly, before they could explain the situation...then there was hope of escape in all the confusion.

Gahiji burst into Masud and Hamadi's quarters, almost tripping on the frayed rug spread out across the dirt floor. Both men jerked awake in their bedding, throwing aside blankets and exclaiming in surprise at his rushed intrusion.

"What are you doing here? You're supposed to be working on the other side of the airbase!" Masud hissed at him in the dark.

"Brothers, I've been discovered by Englishmen who were being kept hidden in one of the hangars all day today. They must be special, to be so hidden, but I got too close. Three of them follow me, close upon my heels. I need help, my friends!" he explained, breathless.

Hamadi hammered his fist into his pillow. "Fool, you brought them here! Instead of betraying just yourself, you've betrayed all of us!"

"There is no time to blame me now!" Gahiji pleaded. "They will be here in moments. We must kill them quickly, and slip away in the madness that follows. It is the only way!"

Masud glanced at his friend, his jaw clenched. The two men nodded, and Hamadi rolled out of his bedding, then flipped the blankets back. Scrabbling in the dirt for a few moments, he pulled a leather-wrapped bundle out of the ground. He pulled a string and undid the knot holding the bundle together, then flipped it open to reveal several metallic objects that glinted in the moonlight coming in through the doorway.

"Brothers, choose your weapons."

SEVEN

Mersa Matruh Airbase
October 28th, 2120 Hours

"Where'd that little blighter run off to?" Nelson gasped.

Lynch shook his head, hands on his knees, lungs working like a set of bellows to force air into his body. The three Commandos had just popped out into a street after following their quarry between two buildings, when suddenly there was no trace of him. The three men scanned the area around them, peering into the shadows around every building, into every window and doorway. They were standing between two warehouses, and the street before them opened up into an area that was clearly meant as housing for many of the Egyptian workers. Ramshackle one-room huts lined the other side of the street, extending off into the darkness in both directions.

Bowen pointed to the hovel across from where they stood. "Look, an open doorw--"

There was the familiar flash and crack of a pistol shot from inside the doorway. Reflexes immediately took over and the three Commandos hit the dirt, hands immediately drawing their pistols.

"And you two thought I was being paranoid," Bowen said.

Nelson grunted and racked the slide of his .45 automatic. "Shut it, you git, and open fire!"

The Commandos brought up their pistols and fired off three aimed shots apiece. There was a cry from the doorway and a shot that went high, the bullet striking the building next to them ten feet above their heads. An instant later, the dark form of a body slumped out of the doorway and into the street.

"Got the bastard," Nelson said, raising himself to one knee.

Lynch moved to rise as well, only to see the glint of moonlight off the barrel of a revolver as it poked through a window to the right of the doorway. He reached out and grabbed Nelson, pulling him to the ground just as a bullet whined overhead, passing through where Nelson had been just a moment before.

"There's more than one!" Lynch shouted.

"Brilliant observation!" Bowen replied. "Let's get behind some cover!"

The three men scrambled back on their bellies until they had the corner of a building between them and the shack containing their adversary. Another bullet tore through the wooden siding near them, and a third soon followed.

"Two different guns," Bowen said. "There's two of them in there."

Lynch nodded. "Alright now, here's our move. Rhys, you lay down cover fire from the corner, while me and Harry break left and make a dash across the street. Once we're out of their firing arc, we'll take the building high and low, while you keep an eye out for a runner. What say you?"

The two other men nodded, their expressions determined. Bowen took a moment to reload his pistol, he was the only one who'd been paranoid enough to bring extra ammunition with him. When the Welshman shrugged in apology to his squadmates, Nelson merely shook his head.

"If we can't sort out these two buggers with what we've got left, the Lieutenant should have us returned to our old units."

Lynch and Nelson gathered themselves to make their run, when suddenly Lynch put out a hand. "Harry, hold on a moment."

"Go, don't go, make up your bloody mind!" Nelson hissed.

"These are spies, eh? We ought to take one alive, so we should," Lynch replied.

"Bloody brilliant," Nelson grumbled. "I'll leave that to you. I'll be shooting to keep meself unperforated with bullets."

"Are you two staying or going?" Bowen asked, steadying himself at the corner of the building. No more shots had been fired for a few seconds, and that made him nervous.

Lynch and Nelson nodded to Bowen, who eased himself around the corner and immediately began firing at a deliberate pace of one shot a second. As soon as he opened fire, the other two Commandos took off at a dead sprint, crossing the street at a diagonal.

The flash of a gun muzzle lit up the window next to the hovel's door. Bowen shifted his fire to the shooter, who ducked back away from the window as the sill splintered from the impact of one of Bowen's bullets. Nelson and Lynch both fired a single round apiece towards the general direction of the front of the building before skidding to a stop at the building's corner.

"Still alive?" Nelson whispered to Lynch.

"Aye, too bad for you," he replied. "I'll go low, you go high?"

"Typical Irishman, mucking about in the dirt," Nelson shot back with a grin.

They crept up next to the open doorway, pistols at the ready. A body sprawled in the dirt at their feet, a dark pool of blood soaking into the ground around the man's neck, a battered-looking .38 calibre revolver held in his limp hand. An alarm was sounding from someplace nearby, as well as shouting and whistle-blowing. There would be armed patrols descending on them at any moment, and if they were going to do this, they had to clear the hut now, before the watch arrived and asked a hundred questions from behind the muzzles of their rifles, while the spies crept away laughing. Nelson impatiently tapped Lynch on the shoulder, and moving as one, the two Commandos flowed through the door, Nelson standing high, his pistol raised to eye level, while Lynch went through the door at a low crouch.

As soon as the two men passed through the doorway, one of the gunmen fired at them. The muzzle flashes lit up the shooter; a skinny Egyptian man, older than their runner, crouching in the far corner of the hovel and blasting away with a small pistol. Nelson immediately fired two shots, both catching the man high in the chest and flipping him onto his back where he lay feebly thrashing, tangled in a pile of bedding. Nelson fired a last, single shot into the man's head, and the Egyptian finally lay still.

Having cleared the doorway, Lynch took a step to the right, while Nelson moved to the left. Lynch's ears were ringing after all the gunfire in such a small space, and he didn't hear the man moving to his right until he felt a body slam into him, sprawling him across the inside of the threshold. Lynch rolled, bringing his pistol around, knowing with a sense of dread that he was going to be too slow, but his attacker wasn't trying for a shot; he jumped Lynch's body and made to sprint through the doorway, only to catch his feet on the legs of the dead man outside the door. The Egyptian let out a cry and tumbled into the dust.

Lynch scrambled to his feet and turned towards the door, his gun at the ready, only to find the tip of a long, sharp bayonet prodding his chest. He saw the bayonet was attached to the muzzle of a Lee-Enfield rifle, and his eyes followed the length of the rifle, coming to rest on a man in Eighth Army battledress and wearing a helmet.

"Easy now, son," the man spoke softly, the rifle steady in his hands. "Make one wrong move, and I'm sticking this bayonet out your spine."

EIGHT

Mersa Matruh Airbase
October 28th, 2230 Hours

"The man's name is Hamadi," Abercrombie said, stepping into his office and walking to his desk, then pouring himself a glass of Scotch. "He's been on this base since war broke out, and he's been spying on us the entire time."

Lynch, Nelson, and Bowen stood in Abercrombie's office, as well as Captain Eldred, Lieutenant Price, and Sergeant McTeague. They'd been there ever since the three Commandos were released from the Eighth Army patrol who'd found them. Although two of the Egyptians were dead, the third had been taken alive, knocked momentarily senseless by the butt of a rifle. Lynch had overheard earlier that Hamadi was the first spy they'd captured alive in Mersa Matruh, and he believed Abercrombie intended to make the most of his windfall.

The Egyptian was being interrogated in a room down in the basement. Abercrombie had at his disposal a couple of hard-knuckled lads who didn't mind roughing someone up on orders. Lynch recalled memories of being locked up in the bowels of Johann Faust's SS headquarters in Calais,

75

tied to a chair and beaten for hours next to the corpse of his squadmate. While Lynch didn't have any real sympathy for Hamadi, he could all too easily imagine what the Egyptian was going through right now, and the thought gave him a cold knot in the base of his stomach.

"So, where do we go from here?" Captain Eldred asked.

Abercrombie tossed back half the contents of his tumbler in one swallow and thought for a moment, choosing his words. "Hamadi has given us a name, one Salih El Haddad. Haddad is a businessman, a merchant known for being able to acquire rare or hard to find items, if one is willing to pay the price commanded by his talents."

"You mean," Price interjected, "he's a smuggler."

Abercrombie nodded. "Precisely. He was involved in the black market long before the war started, and he's no doubt making the most of it - we guess he's got a tidy business in trafficking stolen British military goods. This base sees food, petrol, and even light munitions disappear with some regularity. It is, of course, the cost of operating out of an area such as this, with a poor indigenous population that'll steal the shoes off your feet if you don't nap with one eye open."

"So you've known about him?" Eldred asked.

"We knew he was a smuggler, yes," Abercrombie replied. "In these parts, it's practically a legitimate enterprise. However, we've only kept a light touch on him these past few months. You never know when someone with underworld connections such as Haddad's might come in handy."

"It appears the Germans agreed with you," Price said. "The question is, what do we do about him, now that we know the truth?"

"Word of the shooting will have already reached Haddad," Abercrombie said with a shrug. "It's truly remarkable how fast news can travel beyond the perimeter of the base. What we don't know, is whether Haddad will understand the incident for what it was, and if he'll learn we have one of his men."

Lynch and Nelson had been held at bayonet-point for some time, while the officer commanding the watch arrived on the scene to take statements. Dressed as regular Eighth Army soldiers, and not wanting to give away any details of who they were or why they were in Mersa Matruh, the two Commandos remained silent. Bowen, hidden in the shadows across the street, had seen his two squadmates get caught. The sniper took off at a dead run back across the airfield, to alert one of the Commando officers of what had happened. By the time everything was sorted out, the scene of the shootout had attracted quite a crowd, both British and Egyptian. There was little doubt in anyone's mind that someone in the crowd was working for Haddad and the Germans.

"And if he figures out that we're aware of his espionage activities?" Price asked.

"Then he'll shut his operation down, destroy all the evidence of his collusion, and plead ignorance. We might disrupt his smuggling operations for a short while, but soon enough it'll be business as usual," Abercrombie replied.

Captain Eldred shook his head. "Unacceptable. Regardless of all that, he's certainly going to let the Germans know that something here on this base is afoot. Even if he doesn't have all the details, giving Jerry any advance warning compromises the security of our operation. If he's passing them information, Haddad clearly has the means to regularly get word to the Germans. Does he have a wireless?"

Abercrombie thought for a moment. "He very well might. He lives in a large walled compound to the northeast of the city along the beach. It's big enough to conceal a sizable wireless hut, and if they are clever enough to disguise their messages and keep them short, we'd not pick it up for some time. And that's in addition to whatever couriers or other, more traditional methods he has at his disposal."

Sergeant McTeague cleared his throat. "Beggin' yer pardon, sirs. But the lads and I could hit this bloke fast and hard, be over the walls and knockin' him in the gob before he's even out of bed."

Price and Eldred exchanged looks. The older officer turned to the three corporals standing next to McTeague. "Well lads, care for another late-night adventure?"

Lynch, Nelson, and Bowen all snapped up straight and saluted.

"Sneaking about in the middle of the night through a blacked-out city to kick some dirty bastard right in the bollocks? Old hat for us now, Captain," Nelson replied with a nod.

Price looked at Abercrombie with a smile. "We *have* done this kind of thing a time or two, Captain."

Abercrombie clapped his hands together, a broad grin splitting his features. "Splendid! I do believe this calls for a drink."

NINE

The Outskirts of Mersa Matruh
October 28th, 2345 Hours

Lynch winced and muttered a curse as the Bedford jolted and rattled its way along the darkened streets of Mersa Matruh, sending dogs, cats, and several Egyptians scurrying out of the way. With headlights doused and blackout conditions in effect, the driver was navigating solely by moonlight. It was a perilous situation given that, as far as Lynch could tell, the driver's feet were apparently made of lead, and the dirt roads throughout the city were no doubt planned and laid by a committee of blind drunkards.

The first lorry was followed by two more driving in dangerously close formation, the bumper of the second Bedford so close, Lynch imagined he could reach out and touch the bonnet. In the back of each Bedford there were eight men, all Commandos armed to the teeth. The canvas covers over the lorries' cargo beds were down to prevent peering eyes from seeing the Commandos, although the flap across the back of each bed was rolled up just enough to let a little moonlight inside.

Captain Eldred had given Price command of this operation, assigning one of the two other Commando squads to accompany Price and his eleven men. The lieutenant, Lynch, and six other men rode in the first lorry, while another eight-man assault element, led by Sergeant Donovan, rode in the second. Bowen and Johnson, as well as McTeague and a new squadmate by the name of Higgins, rode in the third lorry along with two more two-man Bren teams, pulled from the other two squads.

Higgins was one of the four new men assigned to Price after the casualties taken in Calais. Lynch found him to be a friendly, jovial fellow who was quick to laugh and - best of all - always offered to pick up the first round of pints. Higgins was quickly accepted into the squad, especially after he agreed to take on the role of Bren gunner. In each of the last two missions, the squad's Bren gunner had been killed, and the men - Lynch included - who'd survived both Merlimont and Calais looked at the job as just a wee bit cursed. But Higgins volunteered for the position, considering it an honor to fill the role held by two other well-regarded soldiers. Tonight Higgins would work directly with McTeague, the sergeant serving as both Higgins' loader and the section leader. The three Bren teams and the sniper team were going to serve as perimeter security for the assault on Haddad's compound, their firepower ensuring that no one escaped to warn the Germans of the attack.

In Lynch's lorry, Price rode in the back with his men, sitting across from Lynch with his face covered in black cork soot, a Thompson standing on its buttstock between his knees. Nelson was there as well, along with Hall, their medic, White, the squad's signals expert, and the rest of their new squad-mates: Herring, Brooks, and Stilwell. Lynch hadn't spent that much time getting to know Brooks and Stilwell, other than the fact that both men were solid, competent professionals who could shoot fast and straight and carry a ruck without complaining.

Herring, on the other hand, gave Lynch pause. Short and wiry, built much like Bowen, Herring was from the slummier parts of London and had joined the army after the Dunkirk retreat. Lynch found this odd, because Price's unit was always formed from men who'd seen combat in France with the British Expeditionary Force. Herring was the first, and only, man in the squad to have never faced off against the Germans. But when Lynch had brought his concerns to McTeague, the Scotsman had become irritable, and told Lynch in no uncertain terms to keep his nose out of the business of officers and who they picked for their squads.

"If Lieutenant Price finds the man fit to fight alongside the likes of ye," McTeague had growled, "then he's bloody well fit and that's the last of it, d'ye hear me?"

To complicate matters further, as they were boarding the lorries, Price assigned Lynch the role of mother-hen to Herring during the mission, just as Nelson and Hall would look after Brooks and Stilwell. Lynch had checked over Herring's kit, finding everything satisfactory, but noticing that in addition to his Fairbairn-Sykes knife, Herring also carried the sword-bayonet for his Lee Enfield.

"Lieutenant Price doesn't like us carrying bayonets, Herring," Lynch had told the man. "They're too long and cumbersome, either on our rifles or worn on our kit. We've got our pistols and F-S knives for the close-in work."

Herring had just shrugged. "I don't mind carrying both, Corporal. Long bit 'o steel in the hand makes up for being a short fellow like meself."

They were an unconventional unit *within* an unconventional unit, so instead of making an issue of it, Lynch dropped the matter. Price hadn't exactly *forbidden* them from carrying bayonets; he believed that they didn't have a role to play given the way the unit fought, and unlike the other Commandos, Price made sure every one of his men carried a sidearm in addition to his primary weapon.

But now, sitting in the cargo bed of the lorry as it jostled and bounced towards their target, Lynch frowned as he saw Herring produce something metallic from his thigh picket. With a soft *snick* sound, a five-inch blade was suddenly gleaming in his hand.

"Bloody hell, Herring!" Nelson said, jerking in his seat. "Put that bloody toy away before we hit another damn bump and you stick someone in the leg!"

Herring merely shrugged. He spun and rolled the weapon between his fingers for a few seconds before folding the blade back into the switch-knife with a smooth motion that suggested he'd done it thousands of times before. He tucked the knife back into his pocket, making eye contact with Lynch as he did so. The hairs on the back of Lynch's neck stood up, and for a moment he wondered if Price knew something very particular about Herring the rest of them weren't privileged to know.

Suddenly the sound of three hard thumps came from the Bedford's cab. "One minute lads, look alive now," Price informed them.

Lynch ran his hands over his kit one last time. They were travelling light on this mission, weapons and ammunition only. He carried his Thompson submachine gun and a dozen spare 20-round magazines, as well as his Colt .45 automatic and its two spare magazines, four fragmentation grenades, and his own F-S knife. Price, White, and Nelson carried a similar combat load, although Nelson also wore a light pack containing a number of different demolition charges. Hall, Herring, Brooks, and Stilwell carried Lee-Enfield rifles instead of Thompsons, and Hall carried a pack containing potentially life-saving medical supplies. Lynch reflected that this might be the first time he felt Hall's skills could be used to their full potential. In Mersa Matruh, there was a full-fledged military hospital close enough that even a serious wound could be survivable as long as Hall could stabilize the casualty and get them to a surgeon, a journey of minutes instead of days.

The Bedford lurched to a halt, and without hesitation, Lynch jumped clear of the tailgate and landed on his feet, Thompson up and at the ready. All of his stray thoughts were banished by the reality of impending battle.

"Herring, on me. Head up, eyes moving. Let's go," Lynch ordered.

With the dexterity of a cat, Herring was over the tailgate and next to Lynch in a second, his rifle butt tucked into his shoulder, eyes looking over the weapon's sights. Disturbing or not, the lad was fast and handled his weapons with considerable skill.

The Bedfords were parked down a wide side-street between a number of multi-story residences, a hundred yards from where the city of Mersa Matruh ostensibly ended and the open expanse of desert beachfront began. Any closer, and they risked the engines being heard inside Haddad's compound.

Lynch and Herring provided cover at the front of the first Bedford, while the rest of the teams assembled behind them. McTeague and Bowen quickly departed with the other six men of their section, moving at the double out of the alley and towards the edge of the city. Bowen would no doubt find a suitable rooftop that gave him a good view of the compound, while the Bren gunners would set up overlapping fields of fire that would give them coverage across the grounds outside the compound walls. Unlike Bowen, who would be shooting in support of the assault itself, the Bren teams would work to secure the grounds outside. Given the low light and distances involved, it was best to keep their muzzles pointing away from where the Commandos would be operating to avoid any friendly fire incidents.

Once the fire support section departed, the two assault teams moved out, slipping from shadow to shadow as they stalked towards the outskirts of the city. Although there was a blackout order in effect, moving among the homes Lynch could see, here and there, a flicker of lamplight peeking through a window's threadbare curtain. Although the

Commandos were maintaining a commendable degree of silence, the Bedfords had caused a considerable racket, and more than a few curtains and window shutters moved back into place as the Commandos passed.

Although Egypt was a war zone, Mersa Matruh was still nearly a hundred miles from the front lines, and no city-wide alarm had been raised. The Egyptians living here had seen enough British soldiers to tell the difference between Tommies and their enemies, and so Lynch felt that most would just stay away from the windows and hope that, whoever the soldiers were after, they lived far enough away that stray bullets wouldn't pose an immediate danger.

Within minutes, the two assault teams had reached the point where the city ended and the long expanse of white desert beach began, sloping gently several hundred yards down to the dark line of the Mediterranean. Looking back behind them, Lynch could see the moon rising above Mersa Matruh, lending the city a sinister aspect. To the east and west along the beach Lynch could see, off in the distance, a number of large residences, all of them surrounded by white stone walls. This was where the city's wealthy lived, out in the open, with the cool sea breezes keeping the stink of the city away. Even in the moonlight the view was, in a word, breathtaking; the stars reflected off the dark, shimmering water, and the rippling foam at the edge of the surf glowed with a dim phosphorescence, while the white beach sand was turned nearly silver in the moonlight. Lynch imagined how beautiful it must appear during a bright, cloudless day, the water a rippling azure plain. A pang of jealousy struck him in the gut, the reaction of a poor Irish orphan to the privilege of the rich and powerful.

Lynch felt a presence next to him. Turning, he looked down at Herring, who looked at the beachfront homes with a sneer of contempt.

"All of it earned with someone else's blood and sweat. Worthless bastards, the lot o' them," Herring muttered.

"In a few minutes," Lynch replied, "we'll give one of them a little payback."

Price stepped up next to Lynch on his right and motioned for the men to gather around. The Commandos all crouched down, and Price pointed towards the compound ahead and to their right.

"Alright lads, that's Haddad's residence. Six foot walls, armed guards patrolling inside them. Four buildings inside the walls: the main residence, a servants' quarters, a garage, and a fourth building which we think is some kind of storehouse for Haddad's more expensive goods.

"Tommy, you and Herring are going to go over the wall on the east, while Nelson and Brooks take the west. Silence any guards you see and give the all clear. I'll lead the four of us in this section over the wall, and we'll secure the compound here," Price pointed to the southwest corner of the compound, near the garage.

"At that point, Sergeant Donovan, you'll lead your section over the wall, and the two sections will begin to assault the buildings. Donovan's men will split into two four-man teams, each clearing the servant's quarters and the storehouse. At the same time, I'll lead my section in an assault on the main residence itself. Once Donovan's teams have secured their buildings and the main residence has been cleared, we'll use a torch to flash the support section the all-clear. Any questions?"

There were none.

Moving low and slow, Lynch and Herring began to cross the beach towards their side of the compound. Here and there, clumps of brush and weeds sprouted from the white sand, and they used this meager cover when they could. Although the compound lacked guard towers, the storehouse and main residence were both two-story buildings, with windows that looked out onto their approach. Lynch silently prayed that those inside were either asleep or preoccupied with something else.

Like warning Jerry that we've captured one of their spies, he mused.

They reached the base of the wall without incident. Immediately, Herring slung his rifle, and Lynch interlocked his fingers, offering the smaller man a boost up to the top of the wall. With a grunt, Lynch raised Herring up, and the Commando grasped at the top of the wall. Herring jerked and let out a hiss of pain.

"There's broken glass set into the top of the bloody wall, Corporal," he whispered down to Lynch.

"Can you make it up?" Lynch whispered back.

"Aye, but be careful. I cut myself already."

Herring finally managed to get into a crouch at the top of the wall, and offered Lynch a hand, pulling the bigger man up and pointing out where to hold in order to avoid getting sliced by the glass. Not wishing to silhouette themselves any longer than necessary, the two Commandos dropped down onto the ground inside the compound.

Lynch looked around them, scanning the shadows. There didn't seem to be any immediate threat, but the smell of cheap tobacco smoke wafted towards them, and both men saw the glow of lit cigarettes as a pair of sentries slowly approached.

The two men were Egyptian, dressed in light-colored paramilitary uniforms. Their rifles were in their hands, but not at the ready, fingers well away from the triggers. Neither of the men appeared particularly alert; the two were engaged in a whispered debate. Looking around, Lynch saw there was little to conceal them from the sentries, and he knew they'd be spotted before long. Using hand gestures, Lynch signalled to Herring they would crawl across the open ground to the corner of the garage ten yards away.

Holding their weapons in their hands, the two Commandos quickly crawled across the sandy ground. Lynch was sure they must be obvious to the sentries, and feared at any second a shout followed by the impact of a bullet, but they made it to cover without being noticed.

Standing with their backs to the wall of the garage, Lynch peered around the corner. The sentries were close now, only fifteen yards away. Reaching out, he tapped Herring on the shoulder, then tapped the pommel of the man's Fairbairn-Sykes knife. He could see Herring nod, and heard the faint scrape of steel against leather as the man drew his blade. Lynch pulled free his own F-S knife and waited, taking deep, calming breaths. He'd expect to sense more uncertainty or fear from Herring, but the man seemed calm, almost nonchalant in his actions.

The crunch of sand and whispered conversation signalled the arrival of the sentries. Lynch tensed, and as the two men stepped past the corner of the garage, Lynch slipped behind and past the first man and lunged for the second. He reached around the sentry's face and clamped his hand across the man's mouth, jerking him up and back while driving his knife laterally through the sentry's throat, the razor-sharp blade slicing through both sets of carotid arteries. With a grunt of effort, Lynch pushed forward, sawing the knife back and forth, ripping the blade through the sentry's windpipe until it finally tore free in a spray of dark, gleaming blood.

At the same moment, Herring struck. Out of the corner of his eye, Lynch saw the Commando stab out with his long sword-bayonet, thrusting like a fencer, driving the long blade deep into the sentry's lower back and piercing his kidney. The man arched back, mouth open in shock, and Herring sprang in, F-S knife in his other hand, and whipped the blade across the sentry's exposed throat, slashing so deep Lynch heard the blade scrape against bone. The sentry dropped his rifle, falling to his knees while clutching at his ruined throat, then collapsed face-first into the sand, Herring's bayonet still jutting from his back.

His own sentry limp in death, Lynch dragged the body behind the garage, and motioned for Herring to do the same with his kill. After returning to grab their victims' rifles, Lynch grabbed Herring by the sleeve.

"Listen here, boyo. One move, quick and sure, that's it. No flashy tricks, no showing off now. One of these bastards makes a sound, and we're rumbled but good, so we are."

Herring was perfectly still, his eyes fixed on Lynch's hand as it gripped the fabric of his battledress. Slowly, Herring looked up into Lynch's gaze, the smaller man's eyes black pools in the dark, and he nodded to Lynch, not saying a word.

If this is the first time he's had a dead man's blood on his hands, I'm a red-headed Welshman, Lynch thought.

Letting go of Herring's sleeve, Lynch gave the other man's kill a final glance, then checked the bolt on his Thompson.

"Alright, time's wasting. Let's go."

TEN

The Outskirts of Mersa Matruh
October 29th, 0015 Hours

Sergeant Dougal McTeague placed a 30-round Bren magazine in front of him, lining it up next to two other magazines sitting on a brown linen kerchief to keep out dirt and sand. Next to him Trooper Higgins lay hunched behind the Bren light machine gun, the stock tucked into his shoulder, the weapon loaded and ready. McTeague's Thompson lay on his other side, also loaded and ready for action.

The two Commandos were hunkered down behind a rickety bit of sun-bleached wooden fence, apparently set up to somehow separate the city proper from the beachfront. They were a hundred and fifty yards from the walls of Haddad's compound, with a limited view of the grounds inside. Although that gave them poor visibility, their job was to provide perimeter security for the two assault teams, so McTeague wasn't concerned.

Their position was in the center of the three two-man Bren teams, the others twenty yards off to his right and left. Glancing to both sides, McTeague was pleased to see he

94

couldn't spot either team; their sergeants, Donovan and Peabody, had taught them well. Both were good men with considerable combat experience between them, and the three sergeants had considerable respect for each other's reputations. Truth be told, McTeague admitted to himself, it was nice operating for once as a larger unit, with other senior NCOs he could rely on. The three corporals under his command - Lynch, Nelson, and Bowen - were all good men in their own way, but McTeague didn't see any of them in his role as squad sergeant. Bowen was too much of a specialist, and he was too quiet, too u̶n̶a̶s̶s̶u̶m̶i̶n̶g̶. While all the men liked and respected him, McTeague couldn't see Bowen chewing someone out, or bawling out orders in the heat of combat. At the opposite end of the spectrum, Nelson was too brash, too erratic, too driven by his own impulse for havoc and hooliganism. While he could certainly curse and knock heads about with the best of them, he didn't have the tempered nature that made the best non-commissioned officers.

In some ways, Lynch was a good candidate. He seemed to have a talent for working with every member of the team, and he served well in both a leadership role as well as part of a larger unit. His background, however, was a bit unusual. Born of Northern Irish parents, his father killed during the rebellion and his mother thrown in prison, Lynch had been raised in an orphanage before joining the army a couple of years prior to the war. Originally, McTeague had felt some reservations as to how well Lynch would serve under an English officer like Price, but after their capture and escape from Calais, those fears were put to rest. Whatever his opinions about the English, Lynch kept them to himself and focused on the greater enemy.

But there was something in the man, some smouldering fire that McTeague could sense. Lynch was the kind of man who sought out combat because there was an unsettling need to, well, pick a fight. Sure, Nelson and some of the other Commandos were a rowdy lot, much quicker to throw a punch or pull a knife than your average sod, but with Tommy Lynch, he could tell it was something a little darker, a little more violent, deeper below the surface. Men like him were of a breed that thrived during wartime, only to get themselves into a lot of trouble when they came home from campaign.

His thoughts were interrupted by a nudge from Higgins. "Sergeant, do you hear that? Sounds like engines, and they're getting closer."

McTeague brought his head up and listened. Indeed, there was the unmistakable sound of automobile engines, two of them, and they were quickly growing louder. Although Mersa Matruh didn't have a curfew *per se*, if there were two vehicles headed in this direction in the dead of night, they were coming here for no good purpose.

Somewhere above and behind him, McTeague heard the faint warbling of a bird, repeating its call in an odd rhythm. It was Corporal Bowen, and he could see the approaching vehicles, or at least the plumes of dust they were raising as they came close. Bowen's signal meant they were definitely coming in this direction.

"Get ready lad. If they're going to Haddad's compound, we're to stop them before they get inside," McTeague whispered.

"Aye, Sergeant," Higgins replied. He was a good lad, young and eager to earn the respect of his squad mates. McTeague sometimes felt that he himself was the subject of more than a little hero-worship from Higgins. The other men had picked up on this, and they made no bones about keeping McTeague's head from growing too big.

With a roar of acceleration, a battered Mercedes truck came into view, the cargo bed packed with huddled figures. A second truck followed close behind, similarly occupied. McTeague made a brief calculation, guessing that at least a dozen armed men were racing towards Haddad's compound right as sixteen Commandos were trying to sneak inside. The trucks bounced and growled down the sandy road cutting across the beach, and they both turned to approach Haddad's compound.

"That's it, then. Open fire!" McTeague shouted, hoping the other Bren teams could understand him.

If they didn't hear what he said, they certainly understood what to do when Higgins rattled out a six-round burst of .303 calibre slugs towards the first truck. There were several sparks from bullets ricocheting off the truck's bonnet, and then Higgins adjusted his aim, ripping out three more long bursts and running the magazine dry. Immediately, McTeague pulled the empty mag free and slotted home a new one, slapping Higgins on the shoulder. The gunner checked the bolt and began to fire again as the other two Bren teams engaged the vehicles.

The effect of their withering storm of bullets was immediate and decisive. The two trucks slewed and lurched, finally rolling to a stop as those men on board who survived bailed out, seeking what cover they could, either behind the trucks or in some depression in the sand around them. The muzzle flashes from the three Brens immediately drew return fire, and McTeague heard both the single shots of rifles as well as the chatter of machine pistols. Bullets kicked geysers of sand up into the air in front of their position, and several knocked holes in the wooden fence above them.

Other, closer slugs whined and cracked through the air around their heads.

Whoever the newcomers were, they were trained enough not to panic when caught in an ambush. They bailed from the vehicles, knowing that being stuck inside such a big target was a death sentence. Then they sought cover and were now returning fire, hoping to throw off the aim of their ambushers. McTeague swapped out another magazine for Higgins, then grabbed his Thompson. Right on schedule, he saw several dark figures running to the west of his position, attempting to flank the D____ team over there and launch a counterattack. McTeague hoped those men were paying attention, because he had none to spare for them at the moment.

"Blimey, Sergeant!" Higgins shouted over the roar of his weapon. "Do all missions get cocked up like this?"

"If they didn't, lad," he replied, firing a burst from his Thompson, "they wouldn't bloody well send us to do the job!"

ELEVEN

Inside Haddad's Compound
October 29th, 0025 Hours

The moment Lynch heard the hammering of machine guns, he recognized the distinctive sound of the Brens and knew something must have happened outside of the compound. Now, the element of surprise gone, there was nothing for it but to strike as hard and as fast as possible, and hope for the best.

"Herring, time to move it!" Lynch shouted.

They'd just finished clearing the garage when the firing began, and they were concealed inside the garage's side entrance. The door was open a crack, and peering out, Lynch saw lights coming on inside the main house, and he heard the sounds of voices shouting in alarm.

Running his fingers over and inside the open bolt of his Thompson, Lynch made sure no sand or plant matter fouled the mechanism. With a thump of his shoulder he opened the side entrance and ran hard for Haddad's residence, Herring's footfalls sounding right behind him.

A porch light snapped on, illuminating the two Commandos and forcing them to squint against the glare.

Ahead a door slammed open and figures rushed out into the compound, their bodies silhouetted by the light. Muzzle flashes lit their faces as the guards opened fire. Bullets cracked through the air around Lynch, small explosions of dust erupting around his feet as slugs hammered the ground. Lynch leveled his Thompson at the nearest silhouette and squeezed off a short burst. Three .45 calibre slugs chopped into the guard's heart and blew it out his back, painting the whitewashed wall behind him with a spray of crimson. Herring blasted another guard, the high-powered .303 bullet taking off the top of his target's skull.

More weapons roared in the night, this time coming from behind and to Lynch's flanks. Glancing back, Lynch saw other Commandos rushing the house, both men from his squad as well as Sergeant Donovan's. Thompsons and Lee-Enfields roared, riddling the surviving guards with a lethal hail of lead. Within seconds, the porch had been swept clear of any resistance and claimed by the two Commando sections.

Price stepped up next to Lynch and surveyed the men standing with him; it appeared that everyone was present and accounted for. The Commando lieutenant changed magazines in his Thompson and nodded to Sergeant Donovan.

"Sergeant, I want half your section to move to the gate and secure it, in case any of those attackers make it past Dougal and his machine guns. Then hold this entrance with the remainder of your men."

Donovan snapped a quick salute. "Yes, Lieutenant!"

Price turned to Lynch and Nelson. "We'll make our way through the building. Harry, you'll take three men and clear the cellar once we've secured the ground floor. Tommy, you'll come with me and we'll make our way to the top."

Lynch and Nelson nodded.

"Those of you with rifles, sling them and use sidearms," Price ordered. "No grenades unless I give the order, and beware of non-combatants. There may be women and children present."

The men around Price all nodded. Herring, Hall, Brooks, and Stilwell slung their rifles behind their backs, then drew their .45 automatics, each man chambering a round and looking at each other for a moment, confirming their readiness. Price gave them all a final nod.

"Right lads, quick and careful now," he said.

Not an officer who shirked away from danger, Price was the first man through the door, followed by the other three men carrying Thompsons. They swept the foyer inside the doorway with the muzzles of their weapons, searching for any threat. But the room was clear, save for several pieces of expensive art hanging on the walls, all of them damaged in one fashion or another by the fusillade that had cut down the guards a moment ago.

The eight Commandos moved through the first floor rooms, methodically hunting for any signs of hidden defenders, but the search was fruitless. Locating the cellar entrance, Nelson led his team down the stairs, weapons at the ready. Lynch found himself tensed, waiting for the sounds of gunfire or an explosion that signalled the injury or death of his friends, but after a long moment, Nelson hollered an all-clear up the stairs.

"Corporal, look for any hidden tunnels or passages," Price shouted down to Nelson, "and then follow us upstairs."

Price turned to Lynch. "Haddad must be hiding above us."

"Aye, time to end this," Lynch replied with a nod.

As the Commandos approached the main staircase, the first resistance inside the residence came from the barrels of a sawed-off shotgun. The blast of lead shot chipped and scratched the marble floor at the base of the stairs, sending flattened pellets ricocheting everywhere, one ripping through the edge of Lynch's sleeve. He had seen the weapon's muzzles a moment before the deafening blast, the twin barrels thrust around the corner of the stairwell by someone standing at the top of the stairs. The Commandos took cover behind an interior wall, and Lynch turned to Price.

"I could cook a grenade a wee bit, get it onto the top landing just as it blows," Lynch offered.

Price shook his head. "The blast could rip through an interior wall and kill an innocent."

"I'll do this," Herring offered, stepping up. "I'll tempt him into firing again, and rush the stairs before he's reloaded."

"And if there's more than one of them at the top of those stairs?" Lynch countered.

Herring shrugged and waggled the Colt automatic in his hand, "I've got seven bullets."

Lynch pulled his own pistol from its holster, chambering a round. He handed it to Herring.

"Now you've got fourteen. Give me your rifle, it'll slow you down," Lynch replied.

A cocked pistol in each hand, Lynch thought Herring looked like one of the crime-fighters in the American comic books he'd read as a boy. The wiry little Commando dashed out from behind the protective wall, and a heartbeat later there was the double-barreled roar of the shotgun, followed immediately by the whizzing of ricocheting lead shot pattering against the walls and ceiling. Lynch glanced around the wall, half expecting to see Herring thrashing about in an expanding pool of his own blood, but the man was instead halfway up the stairs. As Lynch watched, Herring leaped and slid sideways across the landing, hands thrust out, pistols blazing as bullets from an unseen gunman ripped into the wall above him. Herring rolled and came up on one knee, covering the hall at the top of the stairs with one pistol. After a moment, he gestured for Lynch and the others to come up after him.

Lynch reached the top of the stairs and looked off to the left, towards where Herring had been firing. Two Egyptians were sprawled in the hallway, riddled with bullet holes. Blood, bone and brains covered the walls for several yards down the hallway.

"Bloody good shooting that was!" Lynch exclaimed.

Herring merely shrugged. He flipped Lynch's pistol in his hand and offered it, butt-first. Lynch waved it away.

"Hold onto it until we clear the rest of this place," he said.

Herring nodded and reloaded the pistol while Lynch covered the hallway with his Thompson. A moment later, Price reached the landing with the other Commandos behind him, eyeing the dead men at their feet. Lynch saw that one of the dead men was armed with a long-barreled Mauser pistol, and as more men arrived to cover the hallway, he bent down and picked the Mauser up, feeling the weight of the pistol in his hand. His mind flashed back to a moment during their imprisonment in Calais, when *Standartenführer* Johann Faust had executed poor John Pritchard with a pistol just like the one in Lynch's hand. He and Price had escaped Faust's *Einsatzkommando* headquarters, and then fled through Calais with the other Commandos in a running gun battle against the Germans. Their mission was ostensibly a success, but five good men had died so three French partisans could escape to England.

"Just take the bloody souvenir, Tommy," Nelson chided, jabbing Lynch in the ribs with his thumb.

Lynch looked at his fellow Commando and made a sour face, placing the pistol back down on the floor. Suddenly, a pair of shots rang out from a room at the end of the hallway. Commandos moved to cover the door with their weapons, and both Lynch and Nelson ducked into a crouch and began moving towards the door. But before they could get within ten feet, the door opened a crack and the muzzle of a submachine gun poked out, roaring at them as bullets tore into the walls and raced their way. Lynch and Nelson threw themselves to the floor and returned fire, the heavy slugs from their Thompsons blowing holes right through the heavy oak door and the plaster walls. Over the deafening sound of their weapons Lynch thought he heard a man cry out in pain, and he ceased fire, Nelson following suit a moment later.

"Is anyone wounded?" Price shouted, everyone momentarily deafened by the roar of the three automatic weapons in the confined space of the hallway.

No one had been injured by the surprise attack, and the shooter had stopped firing. Price motioned for Lynch and Nelson to take the door, while Herring and White followed closely behind. As they approached the door, Nelson glanced at Lynch, clearly wondering which of the two of them was going through the door first. Lynch tipped an imaginary hat to Nelson, followed by a deep bow and a sweep of his arm, pointing towards the door.

"Bloody wanker," Nelson muttered. Lynch just grinned.

Taking a moment to load a full magazine, Nelson took several deep breaths, then reared back and kicked the door, slamming the heavy oak back against the wall as he charged through, Thompson up and at the ready. Lynch followed a step behind, breaking left as Nelson broke right, the two of them sweeping the entire space of the room within a couple of heartbeats.

They were in the mansion's master bedroom, opulently furnished and decorated with a tasteful blend of Egyptian and European fashion, a mix of the ancient and traditional with the sophisticated and modern. Wardrobes, an enormous three-mirrored dressing table, and a massive four-poster bed dominated the room. At their feet, a young man in servant's livery coughed up crimson froth, a trio of bloody wounds punched through his chest by one of their Thompsons. An immaculate Bergmann MP-18 machine pistol lay next to him, surrounded by a scattering of spent brass cartridge casings.

At the other end of the room, standing in a corner, Salih El Haddad held a small Walther automatic to the temple of a young servant girl as tears streamed down her face. Haddad was dressed in an expensive European suit, several gold rings on his fingers, a delicate gold watch on his wrist. The men had all been shown Haddad's picture before the operation to ensure his capture if at all possible. He was tall and lean, his jet-black hair slicked back from his forehead, a thin moustache across his lip. Haddad looked like he could be an American movie star, sleek and charming, if it weren't for the cruelty in his expression and the sneer of contempt he showed both the Commandos and the girl he held at gunpoint. At his feet, another, older female servant lay sprawled in death, a pair of small bullet wounds in her chest.

"Stay where you are, or the girl dies!" Haddad commanded.

Price stepped into the room between Lynch and Nelson, his Thompson's muzzle lowered. "Really now?" the lieutenant said. "My good man, how terribly unoriginal."

Haddad's brow furrowed in anger. "Do not mock me, Englishman! I'll blow this girl's brains all over the room if you or your men come any closer!"

Price considered this for a moment. "Mister Salih El Haddad, you are suspected of committing espionage, of passing information on British activities to the enemy. What do you have to say for yourself?"

Haddad spat at them from across the room.

"We can only assume informants in the city brought you the news of a gunfight at the base that killed several Egyptians," Price continued. "You might have suspected that the Egyptians killed were some of your spies. Did you pass word of this on to the Germans? Do they know we're aware of your activities?"

"I'll tell you nothing!" Haddad growled. "I hope Adolf Hitler burns your pathetic island to ashes! I hope he takes a piss on the corpses of your king and queen!"

Price's eyes narrowed.

"Very well," Price said softly. "Corporal Lynch?"

"Yes, Lieutenant?" Lynch replied, his eyes never leaving Haddad.

"Make it clean, for her sake."

Lynch raised the muzzle of his Thompson half an inch, steadied the weapon for an instant, and then squeezed the trigger. The submachine gun fired a single shot, the .45 calibre slug punching through Haddad's shocked features just below his right eye, blowing the back of his head all over the expensive wallpaper behind him. Flecks of blood and brain matter sprayed the gold-edged dressing mirrors, leaving tear-shaped pink streaks across their surface.

Haddad's corpse crumpled to the ground behind the servant girl, his pistol tumbling from nerveless fingers. The girl, trembling in terror, reached up and slowly wiped a fleck of blood from her cheek, then turned and let out a shriek of horror at the sight of Haddad's brains slowly sliding down the wall. With a swoon, the girl fainted, sprawling across Haddad's king-sized bed.

"Hysterical bint," Nelson muttered.

TWELVE

Mersa Matruh Airbase
October 29th, 0600 Hours

"Well, that was a bloody disaster!"

Abercrombie stood behind his desk, his face reddened with anger, white-knuckled fists grinding into the tabletop as he leaned forward, stiff-armed. Before him stood Eldred, Price, McTeague, Donovan, Lynch, and Nelson. The Commandos had managed a few hours of fitful sleep before one of Abercrombie's aides fetched them from their hangar a few minutes ago. As usual, the officers looked refreshed and spotless in their uniforms, while Lynch and the other enlisted men still bore smudges of soot and blood on their hands and faces, and their uniforms were still filthy from last night's operation.

"Actually, I believe the mission was a success," Captain Eldred responded, his face showing only mild bemusement. "All of my men survived the action with only a few minor injuries, while the enemy position was secured and their forces neutralized."

Lynch knew Eldred was being a bit flippant, but he had to agree with the captain. McTeague's section had wiped out the two truckloads of men racing to Haddad's compound in a short but vicious firefight along the beach. Within the compound, their two sections had killed or wounded over a dozen armed guards and servants, while a handful of non-combatants were captured. Those survivors were being interrogated somewhere nearby. In purely military terms, their assault had been a smashing success, with only a couple of lightly-wounded men injured by the broken glass along the compound wall and bits of flying wood, stone, or bullet fragments.

Abercrombie, however, was not amused by Eldred's answer. "Don't play dumb with me, Captain. Your job was to capture Haddad, so we could learn what he knew and discover who his contacts were in the city. All that knowledge died with him."

Eldred's only reaction was to raise his eyebrows. "These men are not constables or detectives, Abercrombie. They're trained for swift, surgical assaults relying on extreme violence to overwhelm the enemy. They don't go about with magnifying glasses and notebooks, licking their pencil tips and scribbling down clues."

"That doesn't mean they can't avoid killing one damn Egyptian!" Abercrombie retorted.

Price cleared his throat. "To be fair, Captain, Haddad was not coming along quietly, and he had an innocent woman at gunpoint. He would have shot her dead if we'd tried to take him by force."

Abercrombie sneered. "Endangering your entire mission here in Egypt, and possibly all of Operation Crusader as well, for the life of one bloody Egyptian peasant. I was led to believe your men were *professionals*, Lieutenant."

At that, all the Commandos stiffened, their faces darkening with anger. Price leaned forward, his hand unconsciously dropping to his holstered pistol. Eldred reached out and laid a hand on Price's shoulder.

"My men *are* professionals, Captain," Price answered, ignoring Eldred's gesture of restraint. "That is why they don't allow criminals such as Haddad to endanger the lives of innocents. If you felt we weren't up to running your errands, and cleaning up your mess, you were more than welcome to buckle on your kit and lead the assault!"

"*My mess?*" Abercrombie shouted. "Your men were the ones starting gunfights in the middle of the airbase!"

"There wouldn't have been a gunfight in the first place, if you'd done your job and found these spies before we arrived. Or for that matter, if you'd gone ahead and thrown Haddad in a cell when you first suspected him of smuggling. But instead, you decided to try and be clever!"

Lynch saw that Eldred had had enough. The Commando captain stepped forward, putting himself between Price and Abercrombie, his calm demeanor completely absent, replaced now by an expression of indignant anger and exasperation.

"This argument is over," Eldred said flatly. "Captain Abercrombie, *you* requested our deployment here from Scotland, even when there are assets in North Africa that could do our job. *You* agreed to send us after Haddad tonight, even though you've known he was a criminal for months. If you don't like the outcome of our actions, that is unfortunate, but there is no profit in arguing about it now."

The three officers glared at each other for a long moment, before Abercrombie finally let out a long sigh and collapsed back into his chair, rubbing his hands across his face. Reaching into an open drawer, he pulled out his bottle of Scotch and a glass. He held the bottle up as a silent offering.

"A bit early in the day for that, don't you think?" Eldred asked, a note of disapproval in his voice.

Abercrombie let out a snort. "It's not too early if you haven't gone to bed yet."

Pouring himself a generous portion, Abercrombie drank it down in one large gulp. He stared at the bottom of his empty glass for several seconds.

"If Jerry really wants to win the war," Abercrombie mused, "he should forget about bombing London, and focus on destroying our distilleries in Scotland. The whole bloody war effort would grind to a halt, like an engine without sufficient lubricating oil."

McTeague took a half-step forward. "Sir, any news on the three Englishmen we found among the ruffians trying to get into Haddad's compound?"

"As best as we can guess," Abercrombie replied, "the three men were German infiltrators, posing as Eighth Army corporals."

The Commandos let out a collective sigh, but McTeague was clearly the most relieved.

"Bloody hell, that's good to hear," he said. "Finding those lads among the dead, thinking we'd cut down some of our own by mistake...ye cannae know how awful that felt."

"They were wearing Eighth Army uniforms," Price said. "Their weapons and kit were all regulation, they were even wearing identity disks."

"Their disks look very convincing," Abercrombie said. He lifted up three pairs of pressed fibre identity disks from his desk and held them dangling by their strings. "But these are forgeries. Good ones, too. No real telling how long those chaps were among us, poking their noses where they didn't belong. This means much of our planning for Crusader could be compromised."

"Captain," Lynch spoke up for the first time, "do we have any idea what unit the Jerries belonged to?"

Abercrombie put the disks down and thought for a long moment, then reached for his bottle and poured himself another dram, drinking half of it before answering. "We have heard rumors of a secret German unit, designation 'Brandenburg'. They're dedicated to behind-the-lines operations. Not so much like you Commandos, but rather more like saboteurs and assassins, real cloak-and-dagger stuff. Specialized teams with men who speak English, French, and so on, wearing our uniforms, trained to blend in as they slip through our lines and infiltrate our bases in order to cause mischief."

"And you think these dead Germans were some of these Brandenburg men?" Price asked.

Abercrombie nodded. "It makes sense. If I were Rommel, I wouldn't trust the Egyptians I was buying information from to be completely trustworthy. What if we were paying them to feed disinformation back to our enemies? So Jerry sneaks a few of these clever chaps into Mersa Matruh, and has them pretend to be our men. They gather their own intelligence, keep an eye on Haddad, and maybe even commit a little sabotage while they're at it.

116

Sugar in petrol tanks, sand in the crankcases, that sort of rubbish."

"Captain, I wonder if those fellows were sent to Haddad's, not to warn him or rescue him, but to silence him?" Lynch asked.

The room was quiet for a moment. Finally, Abercrombie drained the last of his glass before reaching again for the nearly-empty bottle.

"Either way, Corporal," Abercrombie replied, "I think you can be certain of one thing."

"Sir?"

Abercrombie raised his glass in a salute, eying Lynch over the rim.

"Jerry knows you're coming, old boy. And he'll be ready for you."

THIRTEEN

Mersa Matruh Airbase
October 29th, 0700 Hours

After the debriefing with Abercrombie, the whole of Eldred's command prepared for departure. The men washed up and bolted down their morning bacon, biscuits and tea, then loaded their weapons and equipment onto Bedford transports. The officers decided that time was of the essence, and rather than wait for the Long Range Desert Group patrol to get closer to Mersa Matruh, the Commandos departed, having used the wireless to arrange a rendezvous a long day's drive to the south.

None of the Commandos looked forward to sitting in the bed of a canvas-topped lorry for most of a day, bumping and lurching along a laughable excuse for a desert road, coughing and choking on the dust raised by the lead lorry. But as miserable as it was, every man preferred the jostling and the dust and the cramped space inside the cargo bed to another day's interminable waiting inside the oven of the aircraft hangar. At least on the move, they were doing *something*, not just sitting around, slowly baking over the course of another scorching day while cooped up under lock and key.

After eight hours on the move, the Commandos' convoy of five Bedfords, guarded by a pair of Morris armoured cars, made contact with the LRDG's scout car. The light Chevrolet was manned by a couple of the scruffiest-looking soldiers Lynch had ever seen. The Chevrolet was loaded with boxes of ammunition and food, cans of petrol and water, as well as camouflage netting, tools, and other miscellaneous pieces of kit piled into and hanging from every square inch of the vehicle. The scout car boasted a pintle-mounted Lewis gun, as well as a Thompson and a pair of Lee-Enfields, all three in leather scabbards. In addition, the two Desert Group men wore holstered revolvers and belt knives. Both men were brown as a bean from life under the relentless desert sun, and they sported thick bristly beards. One of the men wore a wide-brimmed canvas hat, while the other wore a native headdress of white cloth covering his head and neck.

After Captain Eldred and Lieutenant Price greeted the LRDG men, the scout car led the convoy on for a dozen miles before turning off the desert track and into a slight depression, where they discovered the rest of the eleven-vehicle unit. The thirty men of V Patrol met the thirty-seven men of Eldred's Commando force, and each unit sized up the other. Although the Commandos were, as a rule, not the sort of soldiers who adhered to parade-ground standards of dress and grooming during a mission, all of the men wore their issued Eighth Army uniforms in a regulation fashion, and all the Commandos were clean-shaven, with close-cropped haircuts. In contrast, not one of the Desert Group men wore a complete regulation Army uniform. Their clothing was a medley of various uniform pieces and differing patterns, mixed heavily with native North African garments, mostly jackets, headdresses, and footgear, although some shirts and trousers were African as well. In addition, many of the men wore a revolver or automatic, often in a hand-tooled leather holster of local manufacture, as well as a knife of some sort. All of them looked like the two soldiers driving the scout car: deeply tanned, lean, raw-boned men with unkempt hair and thick beards, some so dark-complexioned that they could easily have been mistaken for Egyptians if the Commandos didn't know any better.

"Bloody hell," Nelson exclaimed when they first saw the men of V Patrol, "they look more like a band of pirates than soldiers!"

Lynch nodded at the comparison. The Commandos and the men of the Desert Group couldn't look more different, and their desert guides did have a roguish, motley appearance that made Nelson's comment surprisingly accurate.

Bowen hopped down from the back of their Bedford and stretched straight up on his tiptoes, arms in the air. "A pretty spot-on observation, actually. These men roam the deep desert like pirates, far from resupply and even farther from any sizable settlement. They're looking for Jerries or Eyeties, hunting not to attack and destroy, but to observe and report."

"But we're a hundred miles or more from bleedin' anything," Nelson waved his hands around them. "So why the hell would Jerry be motoring about in the middle of nowhere?"

Price walked over as the Commandos disembarked from their transports. He'd overheard Nelson's comment and scratched his chin, smiling as he glanced over at the Desert Group.

"Strategy, of course," Price answered. "Think of the front lines here in North Africa. We face off against the Germans and Italians north of here along a pretty narrow front, maybe thirty or forty miles perpendicular to the coast. To the north of that, in the Med, we're constantly taking a crack at Jerry's supply lines, just as he's after ours, but it's not really feasible to move men or vehicles over the water to engage in combat – too few places to land them where they wouldn't be vulnerable to attack before the landing could be completed.

"On the other hand, here you have thousands of square miles of open desert, almost all of it unoccupied. If you had routes properly studied and mapped, you could move an entire army in a flank march against Jerry's rear echelon and strike before he even knew our forces were on the move. The same goes for our enemies, of course; that clever chap Rommel would love to steal a march on us and pop up from the southern desert to catch us while we're in the middle of afternoon tea.

"So these lads have a twofold mission. On the one hand, they're constantly mapping and gathering intelligence on the terrain, finding paths through the deep desert along which we could bring armour and infantry to strike deep into Libya. On the other hand, they're on the lookout for Jerry trying the same thing, reporting back on any signs of enemy movement or fortification. Here in the deep desert, there are no borders or front lines, just an ocean of rocks and sand."

Lynch thought of the featureless wasteland he'd watched pass by all day out the back of the Bedford. "And we're supposed to find a secret enemy base somewhere in the middle of all this?"

Price smiled and clapped Lynch on the shoulder. "But of course, my dear fellow. The PM has every confidence in your capacity for performing the impossible."

Later that night, Lynch sat on an empty wooden ration box and blew across the rim of his mug, trying to cool the scalding hot tea before he burned his tongue again. This far away from the coastline, the desert nights were even colder than he'd anticipated, and the mug of sweet tea was a welcome relief as the temperature plunged after sundown. Although he still wore the borrowed Eighth Army battledress, Lynch had draped a woolen blanket over his shoulders as a barrier against the night breeze that cut through the uniform's light material as if it offered no protection at all. He saw several of the Desert Group men wearing native coats that hung almost to their ankles, and he envied their warmth.

Lynch looked up from his tea and glanced at the men sitting next to him. Along with Bowen, Lynch sat with Nelson and White around a small fire pit, dug down into the desert sand in order to help hide the flames from any distant observers. While they'd operated in France, their careful use of terrain meant they were often effectively invisible from anyone more than a hundred yards from their position. But out here in the desert, a small campfire could be seen from miles away by a pair of keen eyes. It was also taking some time to adjust to the fact that concealing their vehicles was an almost impossible task. Although the LRDG patrol bivouacked them in a shallow depression about a hundred yards across, there were hills miles away whose summits had a clear line of sight into their encampment. Instinctively, Lynch hunched his shoulders and bowed his head, thinking of mortar bombs or artillery shells screaming in from unseen, imaginary hilltop emplacements

"What's the matter, Tommy? Afraid of the dark?" Nelson teased.

"I don't like being so bloody exposed," Lynch replied. "Nothing but flat sand and the dark for miles all around us. Plays with the mind, so it does."

"First the plane, and now this? Are you sure that pale Irish skin of yours isn't turning a wee bit yellow?" Nelson asked.

A silent shadow blacked out the stars behind Nelson, and a moment later the Commando bolted to his feet with a yelp and a start as a shovel-sized hand rested on his shoulder. Nelson spun and cursed as McTeague stepped into the firelight, his pipe sticking out from the corner of his mouth.

Lynch chuckled at his friend's reaction. "Now who's afraid of the dark, Harry?"

As Nelson settled back down onto the ground, McTeague squatted on his heels among them. The big Scot had his Thompson slung over his shoulder, loaded and ready for action. Lynch's own weapon leaned against his thigh, similarly ready. Although there was likely no one for miles around, all the Commandos had a long gun loaded and within reach.

"Enjoying our first night out under the African sky, lads?" McTeague asked.

Lynch took a moment and looked up. The vast panorama of stars above them was a little disorienting. The bowl of the night sky was unbroken by anything along the entire horizon, and the moon provided a good deal of light, but the stars were what drew the eye. Even in the blacked-out regions of France they'd visited over the course of the last year, Lynch had never seen such a crystal-clear view of the stars.

White drummed his fingers on the tin mug in his hands, his face turned skyward. "Rather beautiful sight actually, Sergeant. Like a million diamonds, spilled across black silk."

All the men turned and looked at White, eyebrows raised.

"Well I'll be damned!" Nelson laughed. "Bloody hell, despite the fact that you still look like a bleedin' caveman five minutes after you've shaved, I do believe you've just given us proof you're a skirt!"

White glared at Nelson. Reaching down, he snatched up a small pebble, and with commendable accuracy, lobbed the missile into Nelson's half-full mug of tea. The hot liquid splashed across Nelson's hands and thighs, causing him to jump up and curse as he brushed at his wet uniform.

"You sodding wanker, you've ruined me char!" Nelson growled.

"Serves you right," White fired back. "Just because the rest of you lot are a pack of illiterate savages, it doesn't mean some of us don't enjoy picking up a book of poetry now and then. Plenty of soldiers down through the ages cobbled together a bit of verse on nights like these."

"Oi, don't you be lumping all of us in with this bloody neanderthal!" Lynch replied, jerking his thumb at Nelson.

McTeague just shook his head. Pulling his pipe from his mouth, he stabbed the stem towards Bowen. "Lad, I cannae think how ye manage to stay sane around these idiots."

Bowen just smiled and shrugged. "Well Sergeant, I just remember they're all bigger than I am, meaning they're easier targets, as well as good cover and concealment."

At that, everyone laughed. Nelson refilled his tea, and the mood around the fire returned to a more placid state.

After a few minutes of silence, as the men worked at drinking their tea, Nelson let out a speculative grunt.

"That signify anything?" Bowen asked.

"Odd, ain't it?" Nelson replied. "When I was a wee lad, me mum took me to a museum. Saw me a mummy, I did. One of them royals, the Pharaohs, they's called 'em. Sign said he'd been dead for *four thousand years.* Can you bloody imagine? Them blokes what built the pyramids, they were doin' that when *we* were squattin' in holes dug in the sides of hills an' such."

Lynch nodded. "Greece was old when Rome was young, but Egypt was old when Greece was young. The kings of these lands have been marching armies across this desert since men learned to fight like soldiers, so they have."

"And for what reason?" Bowen mused. He dug his hand into the desert and let the sand trickle through his fingers. "You can't grow food or raise animals here. Can't even find a drop of water. Doesn't seem worth killing over."

McTeague took his pipe from his lips and knocked it out against the edge of his boot before standing up to tower over his men.

"More often than not, lads," he said, "kings don't need a reason to send men off to war. All they really need is an excuse."

With that, McTeague kicked sand over their small fire, putting out the flames.

"Off to ye beds, now, and get some rest. Tomorrow we're hunting Jerries."

FOURTEEN

One Hundred Fifty Miles South of Mersa Matruh
October 30th, 0500 Hours

The strike force rose before the dawn and prepared for battle. Each of the Commandos under Eldred's command cleaned and loaded their personal weapons, and the NCOs in each section looked over the men, their kit, and the heavy weapons and supplies the Commandos had brought with them from England. The LRDG patrol, led by a Captain Clarke, redistributed some of their supplies aboard the Bedfords so that a Commando could ride with each of the patrol's vehicles. Eldred wanted his men to observe Clarke's, not only so the two forces could work better together, but so they could serve as replacements in the event that some of the LRDG vehicle crews became casualties.

That possibility, however, was one Eldred made clear to his men he wanted to avoid at all costs. "The men of the Desert Group have extremely specialized training," he cautioned, "and losses in their ranks are not easily replaced. I don't want to seem as if I am devaluing our own lives, but the role of the Desert Group is to navigate and guide us to our target. They are not - repeat, *not* - to engage the enemy except in self-defense, or if they are ordered to do so by Captain Clarke."

The two Morris armoured cars were to remain with the strike force, although their worth in the coming mission was debatable. Their armaments weren't impressive enough on their own to warrant the cars' presence, but their commanding officer, Captain Moody, felt obliged to offer his services for the duration of the mission. He pointed out that one of his fellow officers, a Lieutenant Lewis, had gone missing with a supply convoy a week earlier, and Moody owed it to his friend to stand fast and support the Commandos.

"The lads and I are looking for payback," Moody said. "And a few more big guns can't hurt."

"No offense old chap," Eldred replied, "but if that's the case, couldn't you have brought guns that were even bigger?"

By the time the sun began to climb into the sky, the strike force, all eighteen vehicles, was on the move. The Chevrolets of the LRDG led the way, followed by the five Bedfords blocked in front and back by the two armoured cars. The convoy stretched for almost half a mile, spread out to keep the amount of choking dust to a minimum, as well as make them a more dispersed and difficult target in case of an air attack.

Lynch was assigned a seat on the second LRDG vehicle in the convoy. Bowen was riding in the scout car several miles ahead of everyone else, contributing his keen eyes to the car's reconnaissance role. Johnson, Bowen's spotter, fretted like a faithful hound that'd been left behind while its master went hunting alone. Lynch felt sorry for Johnson, knowing that the two men trained and fought together as a team to the point where they could communicate entirely without speech, everything conveyed with subtle hand gestures and eye movements. Splitting up such a partnership left each man feeling a bit at sea, but orders were orders.

As for Lynch, he found himself in the company of one Corporal Jack Lawless, the commander of the 30cwt Chevrolet leading the convoy proper. The vehicle normally carried three men, but some fuel cans and ration boxes had been shifted to one of the Bedfords to free up both weight and room enough for Lynch to ride along. The Chevrolet was armed with a Vickers gun on a tall pintle mount to the rear of the vehicle and a Lewis gun at the front passenger's seat. Lawless and the two other men, all New Zealanders like most of the LRDG troops, carried sidearms and kept long guns aboard the vehicle. Nelson's comment about pirates came to mind as Lynch climbed aboard and took in all the weapons, ammunition, and supplies stowed everywhere space could be found.

Lawless noticed Lynch's eyes going wide as he worked to find a comfortable space for his Thompson, pack, and his own backside. "Sorry the old girl's a bit choc-a-block, but any place you can wedge in your bum and kit is fine by us."

Eventually Lynch shoehorned himself in between a petrol can and an ammunition box, trying not to think about what would happen if either were hit by incendiary munitions. Sitting on a ration box, he folded his bedroll into a makeshift seat cushion, crammed his pack behind him, and found a place where he could wedge the stock of his Thompson so the weapon wouldn't rattle around. Lawless looked back and nodded his approval.

"Like a natural, you are! By the way, this here's Budgie and Nichols." Lawless pointed to the men in the front passenger seat and back seat, respectively.

Lynch shook each man's hand. "Tommy Lynch, good to meet you lads."

As Lawless put the Chevrolet in gear and began leading the rest of the convoy out of their encampment, Budgie turned around in his seat to talk to Lynch.

"So, Tommy, what regiment d'you come from? Before the Commandos, I mean," he asked.

"I was in the Royal Irish Fusiliers, joined up and served for a little while before shipping out with the BEF," Lynch explained. "Got knocked about a bit in France, then made if off the beach at Dunkirk with the rest of the lads, so we did."

"Got stuck in with Jerry while you were over there, eh?" Nichols asked him.

"Aye, so I did, now. We were torn up for sure at Arras, but most of the RIF made it out of France. Bloody Fritzes and their panzers! But I suppose you lads have your share of panzers out here?"

Budgie nodded. "Your old friend Erwin moved his rolling circus into Libya and proceeded to entertain us for a while. But, I suppose it's more interesting than sitting back home and herding sheep!"

"You're forgetting," Nichols piped up, "there might be shepherding back home, but there's also skirts to chase!"

"Nichols old son," Lawless interjected, "I thought you couldn't tell the difference!"

They all broke into laughter, Lynch included, and soon it was clear that Lynch's outsider status was no longer a concern to the New Zealanders.

As the sun climbed higher in the sky, Lynch experienced the unbridled fury of the daytime desert for the first time. Unprotected by a tin roof or a canvas cargo cover, his skin felt like it was being seared by a blowtorch, and the thick shock of black hair on his head absorbed so much heat, he felt like his brain was boiling inside his skull. Fearing ridicule from the New Zealanders, Lynch tried to remain stalwart, but by mid-morning it was clear that he was suffering terribly. Nichols rummaged around in one of the packs lashed down near at hand and produced a floppy canvas hat, which Lynch gratefully accepted. Nichols also found him a lightweight long-sleeved shirt to wear that covered up his bare arms, which were now turning a decidedly dangerous shade of bright pink.

"Ain't going to be of any use to us or anyone else if you're passed out from bloody heat-stroke before afternoon tea time," Nichols advised.

The extra protection helped, as did drinking a full pint of water. The LRDG men were trained to survive in the desert on only six pints of water a day for all purposes, a restriction brought on by the limitations of operating on their own for extended periods of time without resupply, carrying everything they needed in their vehicles. But on this mission, not only were their supplies bolstered by the extra cargo space aboard the Commandos' transports, but they were operating relatively close to both their own headquarters at the Siwa Oasis and the Jerabub Oasis. For the first time in some months, the Desert Group men could relax their restrictions on water usage...at least a little bit.

And they also understood that although the Commando troops were tough, fit soldiers, they weren't prepared for the harsh conditions encountered during deep desert operations.

As his suffering lessened slightly, Lynch found himself better able to observe his newfound brothers in arms and how they operated. The scout car, several miles ahead of the others, served as the trailblazer, finding sand that would bear the weight of the other vehicles and provide sufficient traction to avoid someone getting stuck. The vehicles that followed the scout car drove along the scout's trail, often trying to keep their wheels in the scout's tracks.

While operating the vehicle was the job of the driver, the other crew weren't simply along for the ride. Lynch saw that Budgie kept a record of their speed, bearing and travel time in a log book. Instead of a regular compass, Budgie used a very complex-looking sundial, mounted next to him on the dashboard. Using the sundial and his pocket watch to judge their bearing, he kept a map constantly updated with their closest approximate location.

"Does every car maintain its own map?" Lynch asked.

"You have to," Budgie replied. "There's always the possibility you could be separated from the rest of the patrol. If that happens, and you don't know where you are, you're vulture food."

While Budgie maintained the map, Nichols kept his head on a swivel with a pair of field glasses, constantly scanning both the horizon and the sky for any signs of the enemy.

"If we spot a Jerry plane," he advised Lunch, "we hide first, fight last. We'll try and get the camouflage netting in place and hope we're not spotted. The desert's a bloody big place from a mile in the air, and if our profile's broken up a bit, those Jerry bastards will have a devil of a time spotting us."

"And what do we do now, if we are spotted?" Lynch asked.

Nichols patted the pintle-mounted Vickers gun next to them. "Then we find out just how ducky my aim is, at least if the idiots try to get within a half-mile of us."

"What're the chances of anyone shooting down a Storch?" Lynch asked, referring to the German reconnaissance plane.

"About a thousand to one," Nichols replied with a grin. "But at least we'll feel better."

Lynch refrained from pointing out that during the retreat to Dunkirk, he and many other infantrymen had taken potshots with rifles and Brens at the attacking Stukas. It had done little to make them feel better while they were being bombed and strafed with impunity.

Morning turned to afternoon, and the strike force steadily approached the Libyan border. Lynch had fallen into a near-stupor after their midday meal and water ration, so it wasn't until Nichols reached over and shook his arm that Lynch realized the New Zealanders had spotted something. Looking up, Lynch saw a dust plume and a fast-approaching speck on the horizon.

"Jerries?" he asked Budgie, who was observing the vehicle through a pair of field glasses.

"Yes and no," Budgie replied. "That's the scout car, coming back at top speed. But there's only one reason they'd be moving so fast and leaving that kind of plume in the sky."

Lynch immediately knew the answer. "Aye. We've been rumbled."

FIFTEEN

Thirty Miles North-East of Jerabub Oasis
October 30th, 1300 Hours

Hauptmann Karl Steiner thumped his fist on the roof of the Autoblinda's turret. "Faster, you lazy turds!" he shouted in Italian at his driver. "We can't lose the element of surprise!"

Steiner reminded himself that here in the desert, where a man could see for miles with the unaided eye, surprise was relative. He'd achieved surprise against the Englishman Lewis' convoy not through being unseen, but by being seen all too easily, and fooling his quarry long enough to lure them in close, where they had no hope of escape or victory.

Now, however, he believed his target wasn't some slow-moving supply convoy, but rather, one of the British long-range scouting patrols, their "Desert Group". He'd heard reports of these motorized patrols poking their noses around his army's flanks, sniffing for vulnerabilities and possible attack routes. Although he'd exchanged fire at a distance with their cars before, he'd never been able to capture one of these men, never mind an entire patrol.

But today, Steiner was out in force, with a half-dozen Italian armoured cars at his command. Fast, with heavy firepower and good armour, the Autoblindas would be more than a match for whatever the Desert Group carried with them.

Besides, the reports he'd read on the activities of this unit seemed to indicate they were largely reconnaissance troops, unwilling to engage in combat and untrained in small, mobile unit battle tactics. He was sure the men were brave enough, of course, but when the Autoblindas' 20mm cannons began to reduce the British vehicles to burning, twisted heaps of scrap metal, they'd capitulate.

It would be, Steiner reasoned, the only civilized thing to do.

Up ahead, the dust plume and distant speck that was the Desert Group's scout car was getting closer: they were slowly but surely catching up to them. Further in the distance, the haze of dust in the air signalled the location of the rest of the patrol. Steiner wondered if the scout car carried a radio: if so, they must have contacted the rest of their patrol and warned them of Steiner's approaching armoured car squadron. Would the patrol even attempt a fight? Or would they immediately flee, perhaps breaking formation and dispersing, so no matter who his squadron followed, they'd only catch part of the patrol? His mind raced with all the possible permutations of the battle to come. It was about time, too. Although he didn't regret capturing Lieutenant Lewis and his men without a fight, the truth was that most of Steiner's time in the desert involved a great deal of boredom. There was so much distance involved, and such small units moving about the desert, that finding the enemy was all too often simply blind luck. Today, they'd been searching for evidence of a Desert Group patrol either coming from or going to their base in Siwa. Thankfully it appeared their luck was good, because only a couple of hours after crossing into Egypt, they'd seen the tell-tale dust plume of the scout car. Steiner had immediately whipped his Italians into a frenzy, hoping to close before being discovered.

Up ahead, it appeared the scout car was going to make a futile effort to lose them behind some low, rocky, sand dunes. The car disappeared, and pushing his officer's cap back and snapping his goggles up onto his forehead, Steiner raised his field glasses and scanned the dunes ahead. At first he saw nothing. Then there was a momentary flash of light as the sun struck something reflective along the ridge of the left-hand dune. Perhaps one of the Desert Group officers was sizing up Steiner's force through field glasses? Steiner imagined the enemy commander calculating the chances of escaping a squadron of armoured cars equipped with autocannons and machine guns.

If you're still standing there right now, Steiner thought, *it is already too late to run.*

Steiner lowered his glasses and ducked down into the crew compartment. He turned to the gunner, who took Steiner's place in the one-man turret to operate the Autoblinda's weapons. "When we close to within five hundred meters, open fire on the ridge of the left-hand sand dune," he ordered.

The gunner opened his mouth to reply, but before he spoke they both flinched as a dozen hammer-blows struck the car's armour plate in rapid succession. The gunner ducked into the body of the car, fingering a bullet hole in the top of his cloth cap. Another half-dozen impacts rattled against the body of the car, and Steiner had to smile at the bravery of the Desert Group soldiers.

Brave, but ultimately futile, Steiner thought to himself. Rifles and light machine guns weren't going to turn away a half-dozen armoured cars. He turned again to the gunner.

"Range to target?" he asked.

"Six hundred metres," the Italian replied, peering through his sights.

"Open fire now, alternating weapons. They need to know what they're up against," Steiner ordered.

The gunner cut loose with a six-round barrage from the 20mm cannon, the whole armoured car shaking with the weapon's recoil. Then he switched to the 8mm Breda machine gun and let off several long bursts, emptying one of the weapon's magazines, before firing the rest of the cannon's twelve-round ammunition clip. As the gunner reloaded his weapons, Steiner peered through his commander's seat vision block. He saw the impacts of the cannon shells on the dune's ridge, great puffs of sand and pulverized rock leaping into the air.

Steiner's radio crackled. "*Car Four to Car One - do we open fire?*"

"All cars," Steiner replied, "prepare to engage the enemy. Lay cover fire along the ridges. Once we are past the dunes, concentrate fire on the vehicles."

Rifle and machine gun bullets continued to patter against the car's hull, but the Autoblindas were effectively immune to small-arms fire. Steiner wondered at the insanity of men who should clearly understand that they couldn't hope to damage the Italian's armour. Only three hundred meters from the gap between the dunes, Steiner squinted through the vision block, searching for any sign of the enemy. He saw movement at the edge of the right-hand sand dune, and he peered through his field glasses, trying to see through the car's restrictive viewport. Although the car's bouncing and jostling made a clear view almost impossible, for just a moment, Steiner could see what attracted his attention, and his blood went cold.

"*Evasive maneuvers!*" he screamed to his driver. "*Evasive man-*"

The car's turret rang like a gigantic bell, and Steiner felt himself get slapped with hot, wet clots of soft matter. His brain vaguely registered it as pulped human tissue. He glanced up and saw what remained of his gunner collapse back into the car. The Italian's torso had effectively disappeared, ripped apart by the impact of an armour-piercing shell and fragments of the car's own armour. There was a fist-sized hole in the turret a few inches below the gunner's optics, and a matching hole in the rear wall of the turret.

Steiner keyed the radio. "*All cars, all cars, we are taking anti-tank fire. Evasive maneouvers!*" he spoke as clearly as possible into the mouthpiece, trying to keep his emotions from distorting the orders and confusing the other car commanders.

There was another immense *clang* as a second shell struck the body of his armoured car, and Steiner felt a tug on his lower leg. Fear rushed through him; he'd heard numerous accounts from those who'd lost limbs and, at the time, only felt a "tug" as a shell or fragment severed their limb in the blink of an eye. Tentative fingers reached down, and to his relief only found a tear in his pant leg and a bloody crease across the side of his calf. But smoke began to seep forward from the engine compartment; the shell had continued through the body of the car and struck something vital in the engine block.

"We're on fire!" the rear driver shouted, panic rising in his voice.

"Driver, stop the car," Steiner ordered. "Everyone bail out!"

There was no way, Steiner told himself, he was going to burn to death inside an Italian armoured car out in the middle of the Libyan desert. As the car slewed to a halt, Steiner grabbed his rucksack, rifle, and map case, then bailed out of the side hatch, followed closely by the front and rear drivers. Outside of the vehicle, Steiner saw wisps of smoke rising out of the engine vents along upper deck of the car.

Bullets continued to ring against the hull, and although Steiner didn't want to be anywhere near the burning corpse of his Autoblinda, there wasn't really any other cover to be found. "Get as low as you can, and don't make yourselves a target!" he warned his men.

Too late. The rear driver went flying backwards as if kicked by a horse, a fist-sized hole blown through his chest. The report of a powerful weapon reached their ears a moment later. *Anti-tank rifle*, Steiner's brain registered. As he and the driver crouched against one of the Autoblinda's wheel wells, Steiner watched as the remaining cars in his squadron charged on, guns blazing, into what he knew to be a very clever trap.

SIXTEEN

Thirty Miles North-East of Jerabub Oasis
October 30th, 1315 Hours

Lynch cycled the bolt of his weapon and shifted his body in the rocky sand along the reverse slope of the dune, trying to get comfortable. He peered through the dust kicked up by the muzzle blast and gave a satisfied grunt when he saw the distant figure lying motionless on the ground. *Sorry about that, boyo.*

Lynch scooted back further from the edge of the ridgeline as cannon and machine gun fire from the Italian armoured cars raised small geysers of sand and rock all around him. Although only his head and the tops of his shoulders were silhouetted above the ridge line, he felt perilously exposed to the incoming fire. One hit from a twenty-millimetre cannon shell and there'd only be half of him left to bury out here in the desert.

The five remaining vehicles in the armoured car squadron were only two hundred yards away now, and over the roar of the Autoblindas' weapons and the sounds of their own small arms, Lynch heard Eldred shout to the men, "*Focus fire on the lead car!*"

Lynch checked his sight picture, corrected slightly, and squeezed the trigger. The Boys anti-tank rifle fired with a spectacular report, raising a huge cloud of dust in front of him as the muzzle blast tore again at the forward slope of the dune. The rifle, all five feet and thirty-five pounds of it, slammed Lynch in the shoulder with sledgehammer force, and he grunted in pain from the impact. Lynch had wisely wadded up a pair of his thickest woolen socks and stuffed them into his shirt behind the Boys' buttstock, but the recoil was still incredible. Lynch worked the weapon's bolt, ejecting the still-smoking cartridge case, and fed another round into the chamber from the five-shot magazine on top of the rifle's receiver.

Calling the Boys a "rifle" was almost a misnomer; it was practically a man-portable cannon, firing a massive .55 calibre armour-piercing bullet. The Boys had been deployed against the Germans in 1940, where the weapon proved to be bitterly ineffective against the armour of the German panzers. On this mission, their likely opponents wouldn't be German and Italian tanks, but armoured cars. And, against those thinner-skinned vehicles, the Boys could lend a decisive advantage.

Which is why Eldred had brought six of them to North Africa.

As the dust cloud in front of Lynch dissipated, he saw his target was still on the move. Closer now, Lynch fired again, and not waiting for the dust to settle from the last shot, estimated his aim and fired a third time.

"Displace!" Herring shouted at him. Assigned as his loader, Herring helped Lynch lift the weapon and they slid down the side of the dune, then scrambled to the left ten yards before taking up another firing position. Lynch saw the car he'd been firing at had stalled out, smoke rising from the engine compartment as crew members bailed out from its hatches, armour-piercing rounds still hammering into the car's hull. Eldred had advocated concentration of fire, and so all the teams were ordered to fire on one target at a time until it was disabled. The crews of the Morris cars had unbolted the Boys rifles from their cars' turrets, and four Boys teams were assigned to each dune; three Commando teams, and a team from one of the armoured cars.

"Next target?" Lynch asked as he settled the rifle onto its bipod.

"Right there," Herring pointed along Lynch's sight picture, at an Autoblinda on the move, its 20mm cannon hammering away at where they'd been a few seconds ago. The ridgeline there was disintegrating under the punishing cannon fire.

Just as Herring pointed out his target, Lynch saw puffs of dust and paint flakes leap from the car's hull, as other Commandos began to engage the armoured car. Their position put them slightly to the car's flank, and Lynch sighted in on the vehicle's engine compartment. He fired twice in rapid succession, thankful that he'd loaded a sixth bullet in the rifle's chamber before the attack. His weapon dry, he and Herring lifted the heavy rifle again and ran towards another firing position, crouching low.

Lynch heard a scream of pain ahead of them, and he looked up to see a Commando from Peabody's squad tumbling down the back of the dune, his uniform sheeted in blood from a huge, ghastly stomach wound. The Commando's teammate was slumped over his weapon, most of his skull missing. The two men had caught a pair of cannon shells. Lynch and Herring glanced at each other and hunched even lower as they ran.

Settling into their new position, Herring stripped the empty magazine from the top of the Boys rifle and locked in a new load of five cartridges. Lynch looked at their previous target over his weapon sights, and saw that the armoured car was in reverse, backing up at high speed out of the killing zone while laying down covering fire with its 8mm Breda machine gun. Anti-tank fire from the other Boys rifles continued to strike the car, and Lynch fired all five rounds in the rifle's magazine as fast as he could cycle the heavy bolt, but the shots were either ineffective, or not effective enough to kill the driver, gunner, or the car's engine. Within a few seconds, the car had retreated, along with two others, out of effective range.

Lynch saw that two of the armoured cars remained within the kill zone, one of them burning fiercely, the other merely sitting still. As he watched, a rifle barrel emerged from the turret hatch of the second car, a white rag tied to the muzzle. Further away, where Lynch had scored his first kill, he saw the two surviving crew members break cover from behind their dead vehicle and climb aboard one of the three retreating cars before they continued their escape, sporadic bursts of cannon and machine gun fire ineffectually lashing the sand dunes and slicing through the air above the Commandos.

"All squads, cease fire!" Eldred shouted, his command repeated up and down the line by Price, McTeague, Donovan, and Peabody. Within seconds the Brens, Boys, and Lee-Enfields stopped firing.

Lynch looked up and down the Commando lines. Behind the other sand dune, he saw a Commando supported by another squadmate limping down the dune, probably with a bullet in his leg. To his left, another Commando was examining his wounded loader, the man's head bleeding freely from a nasty graze. Lynch's mind did the coldly analytical calculations all veterans learned to compute after a battle. Within a couple of minutes, eight Boys rifle teams and one 37mm anti-tank gun had killed three armoured cars and driven away three others, at a cost of two killed and two wounded. All in all, Lynch thought that was a cheap price to pay for their victory, given how easily it could have gone differently.

The three captains, Price, and the NCOs of each squad had discussed how to handle a situation such as this over the course of the last two days. Although the Boys rifles were dangerous to armoured cars at close range, the long distances involved in the desert meant that making such circumstances available to them would be difficult, to say the least. They'd need to lure the enemy into a kill zone where they could be shot up at close range from behind substantial cover, while at the same time not endangering the convoy's vehicles.

In the end a few different scenarios were outlined, and thankfully, there was sufficient cover near at hand when Bowen's scout car spotted the dust plume raised by the Italian armoured cars. Acting as bait, the scout car had approached close enough to give itself away, and when the enemy squadron tried to intercept, the scout car used a tried-and-true battle technique, the feigned retreat, to lure the Italians into a position of vulnerability. The long-ranged small arms fire was used at first to give the impression the LRDG patrol wasn't armed with anything more effective, and only when the Autoblindas were at close range did the Chevrolet equipped with the portee-mounted 37mm anti-tank gun back out of its hiding place just enough to expose the gun and open fire. It had been a calculated risk, but one that apparently paid out a considerable dividend.

Lynch's ears still rang from the Boys' tremendous report, and he didn't hear Bowen coming up the dune behind him. The wiry Commando sniper stood next to Lynch, his scoped rifle cradled in the crook of his arm, and looked out over the battlefield before them.

"Looks like you lot enjoyed yourselves, eh?" Bowen asked.

"So we did," Lynch replied. "Although to be sure, shooting that bloody great rifle is anything but enjoyable."

Bowen bent down and lifted the Boys rifle by its carrying handle, grunting with the effort. "I'm surprised it doesn't come with a gun carriage."

Herring, standing to the other side of Lynch, stared out at the three wrecked Autoblindas. "Heavy or no, they pack quite the punch. Without them, those sodding Eyetie tin cans would have shot us to pieces and ground what's left into the sand."

The other two men followed Herring's gaze. A half-dozen Commandos led by Sergeant Donovan walked out out towards the wrecks, weapons as the ready. They confirmed there were no survivors inside the burning car, but the second vehicle contained two living crew, who emerged with their hands raised, both men sheeted in gore from their dead comrades. While Donovan and several Commandos ransacked the wreck, a lance corporal escorted the two prisoners of war back to where Eldred, Price, Clarke, and Moody were debriefing their men. Having nothing else better to do, Lynch, Bowen, and Herring walked down the dune. Herring helped Lynch carry the heavy anti-tank rifle between them as their feet slipped and slid on the loose rock and sand. As they approached the officers and the prisoners, Lynch saw a crowd of men gathering around. Lynch heard Eldred talking to one of the Commandos, a trooper from Sergeant Peabody's squad.

"I asked 'em, Captain," the Commando said to Eldred, gesturing towards the two Italians. "They's not giving up anything other'n their names and that they're, uh, 'burr soggy Larry', sounds like."

"They're *Bersaglieri*, Trooper," Captain Clarke replied. "Crack Italian light infantry, some of the best soldiers in their army. They're not going to give you anything."

Captain Moody gave a grunt at that, and crossed his arms over his broad chest. He looked at the Italians through hooded eyes. "I think if we knock 'em about a bit, these bastards'll talk to us."

Eldred shook his head. "Abercrombie and his knuckle-men are back in Mersa Matruh, and I'm not going to continue his bad habits out here in the desert. These men fought bravely and stand unbowed, even covered in the blood of dead men. No one is laying a rough hand on these prisoners, understood?"

Moody and Clarke glanced at each other, then looked back at Eldred, nodding. "It's your operation, mate," Clarke answered. "We're just along for the ride."

Lynch studied the *Bersaglieri* prisoners. They were both tall and lean, their skin burned dark by the sun. The men wore long, well-groomed mustaches, and their uniforms, although soaked in blood and crusted with sweat stains, were neatly maintained. Both men stood proud, and showed no sign of fear or concern for their lives while surrounded by men who were doing their best to kill them a few minutes ago. Lynch didn't know anything about these Italians other than what Clarke had said, but he could tell with just a look that they were a definite cut above the common soldier.

Just then, Peabody and the rest of his Commandos returned from searching the Autoblinda, and the sergeant's face was grim. They carried several Italian small arms as well as a couple of other items, one of which was a leather case of the type used to protect field glasses. Peabody walked over to Moody and handed him the case.

"Sir, look at the bottom," Peabody said.

Moody did so, and in an instant his face turned scarlet as his features twisted in rage. His hand dropped to his holster, and he drew his Enfield in a flash, pointing it at the two Italians.

"*What have you done with my mates, you filthy bastards? What've you done with them?*" Moody screamed at the prisoners.

Immediately, Clarke clamped his hand around Moody's wrist, and with some effort he lowered the pistol until it was pointing in a less dangerous direction. "What's the meaning of this?" he demanded.

The armoured car captain handed Clarke the leather case, and Clarke turned it over to look at the underside. From where he stood, Lynch could see there was something stamped into the leather.

"*Lt. James Lewis, 11th Hussars,*" Clarke read aloud. He turned to the Commando who spoke Italian. "Son, ask them the meaning of this. How'd this case come into their possession?"

The trooper repeated the question to the Italians. One of them seemed like he didn't want to reveal anything to his enemies, but the other man, clearly shaken by having Moody's revolver waved in his direction, seemed insistent. Finally the more stubborn Italian capitulated, and the two took turns speaking quickly to the Commando interpreter, who had to slow them down as their story unfolded.

Finally the trooper turned to the officers. "Sirs, they say that a few days ago, they captured a supply convoy headed for Jerabub. They insist none of our boys was hurt or killed. Instead, they have 'em under guard back at their base. The Jerry captain gave those glasses to the car's commander because they were better'n the Eyetie's own pair. Guess they took 'em as spoils of war, or sommat."

The three captains looked at each other in alarm. "Strewth!" Clarke exclaimed. "I think this just became a rescue mission!"

Eldred turned to their translator. "See if Captain Moody's brandishing of a revolver has changed their opinion on giving up the location of their base."

The trooper asked repeatedly, but the Italians had regained their composure, and refused to give up any more information. Despite his earlier agreement, Moody clearly wasn't happy with Eldred's decision regarding the handling of the prisoners. "Regardless of whether we clobber them or not, the fact remains that we have no bloody idea where these blokes are hiding. Trust me, William - it's a bleedin' big desert. We've been out here for a year now, and we've not the vaguest notion of where Jerry and his Eyetie friends might be based."

"I might have found a solution to that," Peabody announced. He was digging through an Italian pack, and he held up a leather map case. He handed the case over to Eldred, who opened it up and pulled out a well-worn map.

Lynch glanced over the Commando captain's shoulder and saw that the map showed an area about two hundred miles to a side, centered along the Libya/Egypt border, with the Mediterranean coastline along the top. There were a few pencil marks here and there, mostly pointing out Allied encampments, but the Libyan side looked frustratingly blank. The Italians, it appeared, were being careful to hide their own operational details in the event the map fell into enemy hands.

Eldred let out a curse. "So much for 'X marks the spot'. There's terrain details, but no sign of their base of operations."

Clarke held out his hand. "May I?" he asked.

Eldred handed over the map. Clarke unfolded the whole map, and then carefully holding the edges, he lifted the map up into the air and towards the sun. A smile crossed his face.

"Clever blokes, but not clever enough. Someone got a little careless using their calipers," Clarke said.

Lynch and several others leaned in close, and after a moment, he saw it; a tiny pinprick of bright sunlight coming through the paper, about thirty miles over the border into Libya.

"Might not be an X," Eldred remarked, "but it's good enough. Time to mount up, lads, and pay Jerry a visit."

SEVENTEEN

Libyan/Egyptian Border
October 30th, 1700 Hours

Four hours after the battle against the Italian armoured car squadron, the convoy reached The Wire. It was, Lynch decided, more impressive than he'd originally expected. The barrier stretched to the north and south as far as the eye could see, a wall of iron stakes and barbed wire almost six feet high and several yards deep, made up of multiple layers of fencing with added barbed wire strands linking the layers together. Without wire cutters, it would be almost impossible to navigate through, and even with a set of cutters it would take a man considerable time to clear a path. The LRDG men with Lynch had explained, as they approached the border, that the Germans and Italians regularly patrolled The Wire, and made repairs almost as fast as the British could cut their way through.

"We've made our way through The Wire a few times," Lawless had said, "and on our return trip several days later, discovered that the Jerries or the Eyeties had come along and tidied up our breach before we returned, so we'd have to cut our way through again. Bloody inconsiderate of them! I'd think they'd be happy to let us go home."

They'd followed the tyre tracks of the retreating Autoblindas to within sight of The Wire, but Clarke had worried that the enemy had booby-trapped their passage across the border, so the convoy had driven a half mile to the north before finding a suitable place to cross. Now, with over fifty men on hand, the job of getting through the barbed wire barrier was accomplished in record time. The Commando squads had brought a half-dozen wire cutters, and each LRDG vehicle carried two. Within ten minutes, a path wide enough to easily accommodate one of the Bedfords was cleared, and five minutes later, the convoy was motoring into Libyan territory.

Lynch noted with some satisfaction that their convoy had grown by one vehicle; the Autoblinda crewed by the men they'd taken prisoner. Although the front driver and commander had been killed by shots from the Boys rifles, the vehicle itself was fully operational, albeit perforated in a dozen places with .55 inch bullet holes. When the vehicle's condition was confirmed, Moody immediately insisted that it be cleaned up and brought along with them. Under the guard of two Commandos, the *Bersaglieri* scrubbed the blood and flesh from the inside of the car using handfuls of sand and a couple of rags wetted with petrol. The stink of death lingered in the vehicle despite the cleaning, and it would no doubt become worse as the sun baked what gore remained in the car's nooks and crannies. But Moody was steadfast on bringing the car with them; its heavier armour and formidable firepower made it worth more than his two Morris armoured cars combined.

Furthermore, the first car to be killed by the LRDG's 37mm cannon had smoldered for a time, but the vehicle never caught fire, and the Commandos were able to strip it of anything valuable, including its radio and both of the 8mm Breda M38 machine guns and their ammunition. Although the Bredas were magazine-fed like the Bren, and lacked buttstocks and bipods, they were operational and no one wanted to leave the extra firepower behind. The heavy clips of 20mm ammunition left in that vehicle had also been taken and loaded aboard the repurposed Autoblinda. Moody had assigned one of his Morris crew members to drive the Italian car, and he took command of the vehicle himself, with one of the Commandos from Donovan's squad assigned as Moody's gunner. It was all very ad-hoc in Lynch's mind, but he was quickly realizing that warfare out here in the desert was just as much about improvisation and ingenuity as any Commando operation, if not more so, given the far harsher conditions.

An hour after crossing the border, Lynch found himself squinting against the setting sun. Budgie, scanning the western horizon with his field glasses, informed Lynch and the others in the Chevrolet that the scout car was returning at speed.

"Do you see a dust plume?" asked Lynch. "Is it another patrol?"

Budgie worked the focus wheel on his field glasses, peering off into the sunset past the scout car. After a few seconds, he let out a scorching curse. "Stop the bloody car, Jack!" he exclaimed.

"What's the matter, old son?" Lawless asked, downshifting and bringing the Chevrolet to a halt.

Budgie pointed towards the horizon. "You should just be able to make it out now."

Lawless and Nichols stared towards where Budgie was pointing, and both men made sounds that indicated they saw what Budgie had spotted. Lynch shaded his eyes from the sun and tried to see what they were concerned about, but he didn't notice anything but a faint haze along the horizon.

"We're in for it now," Nichols muttered, shaking his head.

"Oi, lads!" Lynch said, exasperated. "What's all this now?"

Lawless turned around in his seat and gave Lynch a mirthless smile.

"You're about to get a real crash course in desert survival, mate." he said. "That's a bloody great sandstorm, and it's coming our way."

That night, they experienced what could only be described as an arid desert's form of hell on earth. The vehicles formed a circle and the men of the Desert Group, having more experience in such matters, gave orders to prepare for the arrival of the sandstorm. Exposed mechanisms and weapons were covered, equipment was tied down, and every man fashioned scarves to protect their faces from the blowing dust. As many men as could fit sought shelter inside the three armoured cars, and three men apiece sheltered in the enclosed cabs of the Bedfords. It was decided that as many men as possible, mostly the Commandos, would shelter in the covered cargo beds of the Bedfords. Those who couldn't fit into an enclosed vehicle - mostly volunteers from the Desert Group - constructed shelters made from canvas, staked down and protecting the men hiding along the leeward side of the LRDG's vehicles.

As Lawless and his teammates prepared their shelter, Lynch felt a pang of shame. He found Price directing his squad's preparations.

"Lieutenant," Lynch asked, "permission to seek shelter with the Kiwis."

Price looked at him sharply. "What's the matter?"

Lynch glanced towards Lawless and the other New Zealanders. "I don't want to lose face in front of them. They're a proper bunch of fighting men, so they are, and I don't want to look like a coward by hiding in a lorry while they're out here in the sand."

Price gave Lynch an exasperated look. "Corporal, three dozen Commandos are going to shelter in these Bedfords. They're all brave men. Captain Clarke and his lads understand they're better trained to handle this than we are. You're not going to lose face to anyone."

Lynch nodded, but his face must have given away his reluctance. With a sigh and a wave of his hand, Price dismissed him. Lynch hurried over to where Lawless, Budgie, and Nichols were finishing their preparations.

"Mind if I bivouac with you lads?" Lynch asked.

The three Desert Group men looked at each other, and Nichols gave Lynch a hearty clap on the back.

"Sure thing, mate! Hope you don't mind, but it'll be a bit cozy under the tarp. Keep your goggles on and your scarf tight over your face and ears. I didn't keep my ears covered once, and I was knockin' sand outta 'em for a week after."

Just before he climbed into the sand shelter, Lynch saw Nelson about to step aboard his lorry. The big Englishman saw Lynch looking at him, and shot him a grin and a rude two-fingered gesture. Lynch grinned back and returned the gesture, then climbed inside the shelter.

Minutes later, the leading edge of the sandstorm hit. There was a loud hissing sound, as the blowing sand sheeted across the desert floor and scoured the metal of the vehicles. Puffs of sand and dust made their way underneath the Chevrolet as the men leaned their backs against the vehicle, and the flaps along the side of their shelter let in spurts of dust along the edges. Lynch shifted his backside in the sand and tried to get more comfortable, making sure the cloth he'd wrapped his Thompson in was secure, especially around the muzzle and the bolt.

"Don't fret over it too much, boyo," Lawless told him. "No matter what you do, sand'll still get in. Just strip it and clean it once this is over."

The wind soon picked up some more, and after an hour Lynch wondered whether deafness or insanity would take him first. The stakes holding down the shelter grew loose as the wind whipped at the canvas, and so the men had to use their heels to hold the shelter down, their legs cramping with the strain of digging their heels into the dirt hard enough to keep the canvas from tearing free. The sand caused nighttime to come early, blotting out the setting sun and turning the inside of their shelter pitch black. Finding they couldn't handle the strain of holding down the shelter any longer, Lawless crawled around their feet in the dark, tying the canvas to their boots.

Far worse than the darkness or the rasping dust was the ceaseless howling of the wind and the hissing of the sand. Despite being shoulder to shoulder with Budgie and Nichols, Lynch could barely hear the men when one or the other shouted in his ear; the wind was like the roar of an artillery barrage coming down right on top of them, only the storm never let up, never paused for even an instant. Lynch started to imagine the storm was an unending freight train, roaring over and around them for hours, and only through sheer physical and psychological exhaustion did Lynch finally drift into some kind of fitful sleep.

It was the absence of sound more than the weak sunlight filtering through the canvas tarp that finally woke him. He pulled the goggles from his face, feeling the rim of sand and dust they left on his features, and looked down at himself. An inch-thick layer of sand completely covered him, filling the spaces between him and the two other Desert Group men. There was a moment of irrational panic when Lynch imagined he was trapped under the sand, unable to move, but then he twitched a leg, wiggled his toes, and the small hill of sand covering his legs fell away to reveal the tips of his boots.

Slowly, like the survivors of an avalanche, men emerged from the sand. They stumbled around, looking like pale desert ghosts, dazed and scarcely believing it was over. But the early-morning desert sky was as clear as they'd ever seen it, as if the storm had scoured away any trace of impurity in the atmosphere. The air seemed cleaner as well, purified by the fury of the storm. It was, Lynch reflected, the most beautiful morning he'd yet seen during his brief time in North Africa.

And yet, with that beauty came a terrible price. The three captains did a head count of their men, and with dismay they realized one of the Desert Group men was gone. The two others who'd been with him had no recollection of the man leaving their shelter, but his place was half-filled with sand, meaning he'd gone out into the storm at some point during the night. The squads spread out and swept through the surrounding desert for half an hour, before Clarke and Eldred finally called off the search.

"Poor blighter," Bowen muttered to Lynch as they walked back to their encampment. "Probably thought he could nip out to take a piss, got turned around, and just...wandered off."

"Either that, or he went bloody well insane, listening to that cursed howling wind all night long. Nearly drove me mad too, so it did," Lynch replied.

"About that," Bowen said. "Why did you decide to wait it out with the New Zealanders? They seem like a bunch of good mates, but that couldn't have been much of a picnic."

Lynch gave one final look around them, searching in vain for a man he'd never even spoken to, just one more name on the butcher's bill. At last, he shook his head, and gestured towards their camp.

"It doesn't really matter anymore, does it now? Let's get back and have a cup of char before it's all gone."

Somewhere in that vast expanse of desert, perhaps even right under their feet, a good soldier of the Commonwealth would rest, undisturbed, until the end of time.

EIGHTEEN

The Brandenburger-Bersaglieri Outpost
October 31st, 0700 Hours

The three Autoblindas rolled to a stop, and Steiner was the first man to step foot out of the cars. Stretching, he knuckled his back and twisted his torso from side to side a couple of times to work out the kinks in his spine. When the sandstorm struck, the three cars simply pulled alongside each other, buttoned up, and waited. Some sand made it through the edges of vision ports, and an hours' work was necessary to make sure the engine and weapons were clear of any sand, but the crews' only hardship was a long night sleeping in their seats as the wind howled and the sand hissed against the cars' hulls. Steiner noticed with a frown that the paint had been scoured from several exposed areas along the hull of his car; that'd need attending to, because the bare steel could cause reflections that might give them away to a pair of keen eyes.

Steiner realized he should be more upset about their losses against the British, but he refused to give in to such childish impulses. He'd been careless, allowed himself to be drawn into a well-prepared ambush by a simple ruse. If one

169

of his officers had suffered such a defeat, Steiner knew he'd be tempted to strip them of rank as punishment for their stupidity. Warfare in the desert left no room for mistakes, and frankly, he was lucky they'd escaped at all; if the British had possessed more cannons, if they'd had something more potent than a bunch of obsolete anti-tank rifles, they'd probably have lost the entire squadron due to his poor judgment.

Underestimating the enemy wasn't going to happen again.

Steiner looked up as *Feldwebel* Arno Bauer, the Brandenburger who'd masqueraded as "Archie" when they'd ambushed the British convoy, walked over carrying a mess tin and a cup of coffee.

"You look like you could use some breakfast, *Hauptmann*," Bauer said, glancing at the large bullet holes in the Autoblindas' armour plate.

"What I could use," Steiner replied, "would be the rest of my armoured car squadron. But since I doubt that's on the menu this morning, purloined British rations and some bad coffee will have to do."

"Sir, I am offended!" Bauer said with a tone of humor in his voice. "My coffee might not be up to the standards of the officers' mess, but you've never called it bad before."

Steiner smiled. "I'm just being a bit contrary this morning, Arno. Sleeping in the command seat of an armoured car during a sandstorm will do that. How did everyone fare here, by the way?"

Bauer shrugged. "The British were less than enthused. We tied them up in the back of two transports so they weren't so exposed, but I'm sure it was a rough night nonetheless. For the rest, the Italians and our boys handled it as good soldiers would, with little compliant. The men are busy tending to the vehicles and weapons now. I imagine in an hour, we'll be ready for anything."

Steiner nodded and took the coffee cup from Bauer. He drank half of its steaming contents in one gulp, wincing as the hot liquid passed down his throat. He handed the cup back and took the offered plate, occasionally spooning beans and beef into his mouth as the two men discussed the details of his failed attack.

Finishing his breakfast and looking around, Steiner saw the *Bersaglieri* clearing sand from the engines of their remaining vehicles, while Italians and Germans worked together to make sure the cannons, machine guns, and mortars were ready for battle. The British prisoners had been transferred back to their holding area, and several Italians were serving them breakfast and water rations, all under the watchful eyes of guards carrying Beretta machine pistols.

Although national pride would never let Steiner admit the crack Italian infantry were the equal of *Heer* troops, he had to admit they were the finest non-German infantry he'd ever seen in action. Rommel had performed quite the feat of political acrobatics in order to get these men assigned to his command, and their experience in the desert more than made up for any possible deficiencies they might have as soldiers.

Approaching the British prisoners, Steiner's gaze sought out their officer, Lewis. The man stood, unfed, watching the Italians and making sure every one of his men was taken care of before he took his morning meal. Steiner nodded to himself; Lewis was a good officer, for an *Englander*. Steiner hoped Lewis wouldn't do anything stupid, and that one day, after the war was over, they could meet again as friends.

Lewis saw Steiner approaching. Looking past the German, Lewis noticed there were only three Autoblindas. A faint smile graced his lips.

"It appears you ran into a spot of trouble, Captain," Lewis said. "And your uniform needs a bit of a scrub."

Steiner looked down at his clothes. After escaping the ambush, he'd used sand to scour most of the blood and gore from his uniform, but it was still stained with the remains of his gunner. He'd also torn away his left pant leg at the knee in order to clean and bandage the wound in his calf. *Not exactly ready for the parade grounds*, Steiner thought to himself.

"Yes, make your jokes," he replied to Lewis. "Ten good soldiers are dead or captured, thanks to your comrades in the so-called Desert Group."

The flicker of a frown crossed Lewis' features. It was all the confirmation Steiner needed. "So, that was not the Desert Group we encountered. They must have sent someone else - perhaps a force of your Commando raiders? We are aware of them, of course. If that is the case, the next few days will be more interesting than anything we've experienced out here so far. I have been hoping to do battle against England's finest."

Lewis merely shrugged. "Can't rightly say, Captain. Seems you've come to your own conclusions."

"You're a good soldier, *Herr* Lewis," Steiner said, turning and walking away. "But try not to get *too* clever."

Steiner walked back to Bauer, who was talking with their radio operator a respectful distance away. Steiner handed Bauer his empty plate and took the cup of coffee, finishing it in a couple of swallows. The coffee had cooled to a more comfortable temperature. The radioman saluted and handed Steiner a folded, decoded message. Steiner took a minute to read and digest its contents.

STATION MM COMPROMISED LOCAL ASSETS CAPTURED BEFORE STERILIZATION COULD BE COMPLETED BROTHERS LOST TO ENEMY STRIKE FORCE BE PREPARED FOR ATTACK ON YOUR LOCATION MOST LIKELY BRITISH COMMANDO TROOPS AND MOTORIZED ASSETS USE BEST JUDGEMENT IN HOLDING OR FALLING BACK FROM CURRENT POSITION HEIL HITLER LONG LIVE THE GLORIOUS THIRD REICH

Steiner pointed to the radioman's uniform blouse pocket and the man produced a cigarette lighter. Steiner took it and set fire to the message, which flared to ashes in seconds. He handed the lighter back to the radioman and dismissed him with a salute. As the man walked away, Steiner turned to his *Feldwebel*.

"We've lost our intelligence assets in Mersa Matruh," he told Bauer, "and our infiltration team there has been killed. The British have sent a special unit against us. Commando raiders."

"What are you going to do?" Bauer asked.

"I made a mistake yesterday, and paid for it dearly. They ambushed us with anti-tank rifles and a light cannon. The storm no doubt concealed our tyre tracks, but it is possible they'll find us eventually. We need to be ready when they come for us."

"Do you think they'll have armour?" Bauer asked.

"It's not armour I'm worried about," Steiner replied.

"What then? Artillery? The RAF?"

"No, we can deal with those in one fashion or another," Steiner said a little too quickly. He turned and looked back out over the desert to the east, squinting into the rising sun.

"What concerns me most," Steiner finally answered, "are men who aren't afraid of the dark."

NINETEEN

Five Miles East of the Outpost
October 31st, 1500 Hours

"Got you, you blighters."

Lynch turned and looked at Jack Lawless as the New Zealander handed him the field glasses.

"A few points to the left, that low hill," Lawless said.

The two men lay against the eastern edge of a small sand dune. Several hundred yards behind them, the rest of the convoy had stopped, and other men with field glasses - the three captains and several others - were prone behind other low sand mounds, looking out across the desert towards their target. Bowen and the men in the scout car had spotted the fortress an hour ago, and had waited for the rest of the convoy to arrive, waving them to a halt a mile away so they could approach slowly and reduce their dust plume.

Lynch brought the glasses to his eyes, and in a few seconds, he found their target. The hill was miles away, and if Lawless hadn't given him some idea of where to look, he might have missed the fortress, but the artificial structure was just barely visible; a rectangular bump on the top of a

176

shallow, rocky hill. Between the fortress and their location there were a few small dunes, but nothing large enough to conceal the approach of almost twenty vehicles.

"If they've got a light field gun or some heavy mortars," Lynch muttered, "we'll be bracketed and smashed to pieces before we get within range of anything we're carrying ourselves. And they'll be seeing us long before we're even in range of their guns."

Lawless nodded. "A mug's game for sure. If we had a squadron of A-9s or Crusaders, this might be different. But our girls and your great bloody lumbering oxen would get chopped into buzzard bait by a couple of spandaus, never mind anything heavier. And you bloody well know they've got more than a couple of spandaus up there."

"Three armoured cars, to be sure," Lynch replied. "And this time, we won't be so lucky. Couldn'a get within a thousand yards with those Boys rifles, and at that range, might as well be shooting at those cars with my bloody Thompson."

Both men heard movement and rolled over to see several men from Lynch's squad approaching. Price, McTeague, Nelson, and Bowen walked over to the base of the dune. As the others used their field glasses, Bowen unslung his rifle and climbed up the dune, laying down next to Lynch and peering through the optics of his Lee-Enfield.

Although his sniper scope had lower magnification than Lawless' field glasses, it took Bowen only a moment to grunt in satisfaction as he spotted the enemy base.

"Put me at the top of that fort," he said to no one in particular, "and no one could get within a thousand yards without a bullet in 'em."

"Do you think the Germans have someone with your degree of skill, Corporal?" Price asked mildly.

Bowen shrugged, his eye still peering through the scope. "They don't need a *me*, they just need a good mortar or MG team. There's a mile-wide kill zone around that hill flat as my mother's frying pan. And you know they've got range stakes posted, interlocking fields of fire, beaten zones all mapped out. Jerry is a particularly methodical animal when given a bit of time to dig in, sir."

A meeting between all the officers and their NCOs was held immediately. Clarke, Moody, and Eldred debated strategies for attacking the enemy fort, while Price, along with the Commando, armoured car, and New Zealander non-commissioned officers, mostly listened on, only speaking when asked questions about their men or wargear. Moody favored a swift armoured assault, using the Autoblinda and the two Morris cars to spearhead an attack with the LRDG Chevrolets sweeping in along the flanks, laying down covering fire. Eldred preferred a more infantry-based approach, setting up a base of fire at the extreme range of their support weapons, while working men forward in ones and twos, giving the Germans no easy targets, until they were able to bring the men together for one final assault. Clarke, whose force was trained for reconnaissance rather than combat, advocated a more long-sighted approach. He thought perhaps encircling the fort and radioing for reinforcements, while at the same time preventing a breakout, might be the better bet.

Time passed, and the sun continued to slide towards the western horizon. Finally, when the debate had reached a lull, Price cleared his throat, drawing the attention of the three superior officers.

"No need to be so coy, David," Eldred said. "We're clearly not getting anywhere. Out with it."

"I want to meet him," Price replied.

Moody frowned. "Who?"

Price tipped his head to the west. "Their commanding officer. I want to meet him. We don't know anything about these Germans; we don't know their full strength, or how well-provisioned they are. We don't know if their commanding officer is an unimaginative ass, or if he's going to be a crafty little fox and give us nothing but trouble. We need to know who we're dealing with."

"He's a Brandenburg officer," Eldred replied. "He's not going to be a lock-step Jerry or a bloodthirsty SS dropout. He's going to be a clever bastard, make no mistake."

"I still say we make contact. If he's got half a brain, he'll know we're already out here, somewhere," Price said.

"And you want to confirm his suspicions? You're giving up any element of surprise," Clarke pointed out.

"I think it's worth the risk," Price answered.

The three captains remained silent for a moment. Finally, Eldred let out a short laugh and shook his head. "Durnford-Slater warned me about you, David. Fine, take two men. We're clearly scratching our heads trying to think of anything better to do and failing. If you ask Captain Clarke here nicely, maybe he'll give you the keys to his scout car."

Price turned to look at the New Zealander captain. Clarke rolled his eyes and pointed over his shoulder towards the car with his thumb. "Not so much as a scratch, y'hear mate? Scratch it, and you better not bother coming back."

Price shot him a salute. "Yes, Captain!"

A few feet away, Lynch leaned over to Bowen. "Don't see this turning out very well, so I don't."

Price overheard, and turned to look at the two men. "For your sake, Corporal, I hope you're wrong. Because you're the two chaps I'm bringing with me. Prepare your kit, we're leaving in five minutes."

Half an hour later, the three Commandos sat in the scout car, baking in the late afternoon sun as it beat down on their bodies with a fury that seemed to only increase as the minutes ticked away, and Lynch suspected it was the desert's way of telling them this was a bad idea.

"This was a bad idea," Bowen said. He peered at the fortress through a pair of field glasses, the structure only half a mile away. "We're well within range of a German medium mortar, and practically point-blank range for a light howitzer. One hit and we'll be nothing but scrap metal and rendered meat."

Price had insisted on getting dangerously near to the enemy; he wanted the sniper's keen eye poring over every visible inch of the base while they could get this close. Lynch sat in the driver's seat, his Thompson locked and loaded at his feet. They'd stripped the Lewis gun from its pintle mount as a sign of good faith, replacing it with a large white towel on a spare wireless antenna. Price merely sat in the front passenger seat, his feet propped on the car's dash, and sipped lukewarm tea from his canteen, officer's cap pulled down low over his eyes.

"A bit too late to be second-guessing your superior officer, don't you think?" Price asked Bowen.

"I think you're right, because here they come," Bowen announced.

A few moments later, a dust plume could be seen, growing in size and coming their way. A small vehicle was traveling towards them at high speed, and as the seconds passed, they could see the familiar shape of a German Kübelwagen.

"Did you stop and think now, about the last time we spoke to a Nazi officer?" Lynch asked.

"You mean Faust?" Price replied.

"Aye."

"I think of that moment every day. Don't you?"

"Aye, that I do. And not fondly, either."

"Do you expect things to go the same way right now?"

"Lieutenant, I've learned to expect nothing, and prepare for everything. That's why I've got a loaded Thompson at my feet and a cocked pistol in my hand."

"Well then," Price replied with a smile. "I've nothing to worry about. Look alive now, our guests have arrived."

The Kübelwagen rolled to a stop fifty yards away. They could see three men in the vehicle, and two of them climbed out. One of them was dressed as an Afrika Korps officer, while the other was his sergeant. Both of them wore sidearms, but neither had a weapon at hand.

Price swung his feet down off the dash and began to climb out of the car. "Corporal Bowen, wish us luck, and make sure there's a round in the chamber of your rifle."

Bowen reached over and patted his Lee-Enfield, sitting on the seat next to him. "I've checked three times, sir. Good luck."

"And don't bloody miss, Rhys," Lynch added.

"Do I ever?" Bowen asked.

"Don't start now," Lynch replied.

Lynch stepped out of the car and casually tucked his .45 automatic into the small of his back. He also had a grenade clipped to his belt, just in case. He and Price fell in step together as they approached the Germans, who were also walking forward to meet them halfway. With a sidelong glance, Lynch noted that Price had the flap of his pistol holster undone.

"Do *you* have a round chambered, sir?" Lynch asked.

"Do *you* even have to ask?" Price replied.

Ten feet apart, the two parties stopped. Lynch saw the two men were lean and sun-burnt, appearing much like the men of the Desert Group. Both had the look of veteran fighting men, but while they appeared cautious, neither had the look of disdain or smugness he'd seen so many times in the faces of German soldiers.

Price saluted the German. "Lieutenant David Price, Three Commando."

The German returned Price's salute. "*Hauptmann* Karl Steiner, Regiment Brandenburg."

A long moment passed in silence, and then Steiner cleared his throat. "I must apologize," he said.

"For what?" Price asked.

"For underestimating you yesterday. That was very foolish of me, and it cost me the lives of ten men, as well as three vehicles."

"Two of your men survived the attack."

"You have them under guard?"

"We do. They are being treated fairly. They comported themselves with great discipline, and only admitted to having knowledge of your British prisoners of war after we found the purloined field glasses."

Steiner nodded. "Ah, yes. Lieutenant Lewis. He and his men are well, if a bit more brown than the last time Englishmen laid eyes on them. But their needs are being met. I do not believe in mistreating prisoners."

"I appreciate that. I have had dealings, in the past, with German officers who weren't so professional."

"That is unfortunate. I would apologize for their behavior as well, but if I continue, soon you would have me apologizing for the entire war."

"So, you condone Hitler's actions?"

Steiner glanced down at the dust on his boots. "It is not for a simple soldier such as myself to judge the policies and decisions of my superiors. I will leave it at that."

"Understood."

"Now then," Steiner looked up and met Price's eyes. "I hope you do not insult me by offering terms."

Price shook his head. "I think that would be a little premature. Your position appears quite defensible."

"It is, quite. But I have little knowledge of the forces at your disposal. Perhaps my situation is more desperate than I realize."

Price shrugged. "I imagine I am as ignorant of what you've got up on that hill as you are of my own forces."

"So, why the meeting?"

"This desert is a strange place," Price said, raising a hand and sweeping it across a section of the horizon. "There is nothing here, nothing of value at all except empty space on a map. And yet there is value in that empty space. It is the unlocked gate that lets each of us into the other's backyard."

"It is good to know we're not just here for the suntans, *ja*?" Steiner mused.

Price smiled. "Did you know, in the sixth century B.C., an entire Persian army, fifty thousand strong, vanished

185

without a trace in a sandstorm like the one we endured last night? Somewhere near the Siwa oasis, no more than a hundred miles from here. *Fifty thousand men.* Soldiers just like us, buried by the sands without a trace for two and a half millennia."

"It is a sobering thought," Steiner said. "Do you fear that we shall disappear out here as well? Our two forces struggling in battle to the last man, only to be lost for all time?"

"I don't fear death," Price answered. "But I don't fancy the idea of dying without cause. We're soldiers, yes. But we are also human beings."

"Is that why you wished to meet me? To remind me of our common humanity? That is an unusual philosophy for a war zone."

Price shook his head. "Nothing so maudlin, I assure you. But I've rarely had the chance to hold a conversation with my opponent that wasn't conducted over the muzzle of a gun. It is nice to be reminded that some Germans aren't mindless brutes."

Steiner's eyes hardened a bit. "Do not be so foolish, Lieutenant, as to think I cannot be brutal."

"Brutality is often a necessity in war, Captain. But mindlessness is not." Price stepped forward and extended his hand.

After a moment's hesitation, Steiner accepted the offering with a hearty handshake. "This does not mean I won't try to shoot you sometime soon, Lieutenant."

"I'd be rather offended if you didn't, old bean. Cheers!"

"*Auf Wiedersehen*, Lieutenant."

The two officers turned from each other and began to walk back to their vehicles. Lynch merely nodded to the German sergeant who, like him, hadn't said a word the entire time. The German returned his nod, and then the two men followed their officers.

Back at the car, Bowen was holding the rifle in his lap. "Well, no one's dead, so I'm assuming that went well."

"He seemed to be an agreeable enough chap," Price said as he climbed into the car.

Lynch started the ignition and swung the car around in a wide U-turn, heading back towards their encampment.

"Well now, Lieutenant, do you have a plan?" Lynch asked.

"Of course I do, Tommy," Price answered. "We shall sneak up on the poor buggers in the middle of the night, and then kill them all."

TWENTY

Half a Mile South of the Outpost
October 31st, 2330 Hours

Price's squad approached the enemy outpost, moving slowly and silently in an irregular, staggered formation. Each man carried only his weapons, ammunition, and other bare necessities, everything carefully padded and secured to eliminate the slightest noise or reflection. Each of the men was linked to those in front and back by a twenty-yard length of twine cinched to each man's belt. This provided a silent means of getting the attention of the man in front or behind with a quick tug or two on the line.

At the moment, Lynch walked point, his eyes straining to see as far as possible in the night. Although the sky was clear and he could make out the terrain immediately around him, the bright moon above them bleached more distant features of their color and texture, making it hard to pick out any details. Lynch found that the moonlit rocks and sand played tricks along the corners of his vision, and many times he half-saw movement that turned out to be nothing more than a phantom of the moonlight and his own nerves.

The first few miles had been relatively easy. The squad set out half an hour after sunset on a bearing that would bring them about a mile south of the enemy outpost. Once they'd reached that spot, and the silhouette of the fortress was seen directly below the North Star, they'd changed direction and moved towards the enemy stronghold. This time, however, they moved far slower, spread out randomly so they wouldn't appear as a regular line of shapes at a distance. The squad crept forward with a silent, careful pace, and Lynch employed every bit of his training in night maneuvers to ensure he didn't step on a bit of dry brush or kick a rock while they advanced. The strain of such a state of alertness, coupled with their slow progress, was exhausting. That he and the other Commandos had slept fitfully at best through a raging sandstorm the previous night, and were therefore ill-rested to begin with, did not help matters any.

Lynch glanced over his shoulder and saw the silhouette of Higgins behind him. Lynch noted the large, angular shape of a machine gun hanging at Higgins' chest from a makeshift patrol sling. Price had decided to bring both of the captured Italian machine guns along to provide the squad with as much firepower as possible. Both Higgins and Brooks, another one of the new men, each carried a Breda with their ammunition pouches stuffed with magazines. Stilwell, one of the other new squadmates, served as an ammunition carrier for both men, his haversack bulging with more loaded magazines. McTeague one again took possession of the squad's Bren gun, inviting wry comments from Nelson and Lynch to the effect that McTeague should just give up his rank and remain a squad machine gunner if he was going to wind up carrying the weapon on every mission.

In addition to the two extra light machine guns, Stilwell, Hall, Johnson, and Herring, men who normally carried rifles, were carrying Thompsons tonight. Men of the Desert Group and the armoured car crews willingly exchanged weapons with the Commandos to ensure that every man in the squad had an automatic weapon. Bowen was the lone exception with his scoped Lee-Enfield; it would make little sense for the squad's sniper to give up his most lethal instrument. Lynch knew that Johnson, Bowen's spotter, would do yeoman's work protecting his teammate if the fighting got thick.

Lynch's attention snapped back to the task at hand as his ears detected a faint sound off to his two o'clock. It was the sound of metal on metal, perhaps a trigger guard or bolt handle clinking against a belt buckle. Instantly, Lynch stopped and tugged three times on the twine leading back to Higgins. There was a single return tug of acknowledgement, and Lynch very carefully lowered himself onto his belly.

Looking behind him, he saw the dark outlines of his teammates disappear one by one as they went prone against the desert sand.

Time passed, and Lynch wondered if the sound had been another figment of his overactive imagination. But then, from off to his right, he heard the distinct sound of a boot sole scuffing across a rock. Looking only indirectly towards the sound as he'd been taught during night maneuvers training, he caught the dark outlines of three men moving across his field of view, perhaps a hundred yards away. Lynch heard faint whispers in Italian, the occasional scraping of wood against metal; the sounds of men carrying weapons and equipment on the move. The three-man patrol was maintaining good discipline, although they fell short of Commando standards for night operations.

At first, Lynch thought Price was going to let them pass, but there was a soft tug on the twine to get his attention, and Lynch turned to see another shadow had slipped next to him. It took Lynch a moment to recognize Herring, and the young man leaned in close and put his lips to Lynch's ear.

"Price says we take them. You, me, Nelson. Quiet-like, with blades."

Lynch nodded, his movement felt more than seen against Herring's face. Leaving his Thompson on the

191

ground, he untied himself from the guideline, then rose to a crouch. He looked and saw the low, hulking form of Nelson silently approaching. Herring reached out and tapped Lynch's shoulder, and as one, the three Commandos slipped away from the others and after the Italian patrol.

The stalk took ten minutes, and the *Bersaglieri* died without a sound. The Commandos first matched speed with their quarry, and then with great care, increased their pace just enough to eventually overtake the patrol two hundred yards from where they'd passed by. Each of the Commandos chose a victim and struck from behind with a lightning-quick stab or slash, while free hands clamped over throats or mouths. In a matter of seconds, the three Italians were lowered to the ground with the sort of odd tenderness one normally reserves for a drunken mate after a night of too many pints at the local pub.

The dead were given a perfunctory pat-down, and a few items were pocketed. Lynch tucked a German-made stick grenade into his belt, while he watched Herring deftly pocket a gold-faced watch. Noticing the speed and efficacy with which Herring looted the corpse at his feet, Lynch once again wondered where Herring must have come from, and why Price had allowed him into this squad, without ever having faced the Germans in battle.

Something tells me I don't really want to know, Lynch thought.

In a moment, the men cleaned their knives on the uniforms of the dead, and five minutes later, they were back with the rest of their squad. Weapons were gathered, and without speaking a word the entire time, the twelve men resumed their march towards the hilltop fortress. Lynch pulled open the shirt pocket of his battledress blouse and looked at the luminous dial of his watch. It was almost midnight.

Midnight on All-Hallows' Eve, Lynch thought with a grin. *Time to give Jerry and the Eyeties more than just a fright.*

TWENTY-ONE

The Outpost
November 1st, 0001 Hours

Steiner raised the binoculars to his eyes and scanned the moonlit desert once again, hunting for any man-made shapes or movement. From the firing step atop the fortress wall he could see for kilometres in any direction, but although the sand seemed to glow with the reflection of the bright moonlight, it was impossible to clearly discern features he knew he could pick out easily during the day.

On any other night, Steiner would have been asleep two hours ago, but his encounter with the British Commandos had unsettled him. Knowing the enemy was out there somewhere in the desert, hiding and plotting nearby, kept him from his bed. He was by nature a hunter, a man who needed to have the initiative on his side. Even when he sat waiting to ambush a convoy, lurking like a spider in the center of a web, he felt completely in control of the situation.

But this uncertainty, this waiting in the dark for something to happen, was chipping away at his nerve with disturbing effectiveness. The night was either a soldier's

194

greatest ally or his most dreadful enemy. Either it hid him and protected him from the searching eyes of the opposing side, glaring out from behind the muzzles of their guns, or it conjured all manner of unknown terrors lurking just out of sight. Shells, blades, bullets - any of them could kill from the shadows, striking before their victims knew what hit them. Normally Steiner appreciated the darkness for the freedom it gave him to move and strike unseen, but now that he was on the other end of that equation, a thread of fear coiled in his belly.

And, although he was loathe to admit it to himself, the Commando's story of the long-lost army buried in the desert only added to his uneasiness. Steiner was a soldier, first and foremost, not a Nazi. Although his father had sworn fealty to the party in order to remain a successful businessman, privately the Steiner family had no love for Hitler and his politics.

When war loomed on the horizon, Steiner knew he would find himself in uniform, one way or another. With his fluency in English and his passable Italian and French, he was able to join the Brandenburg regiment and soon found himself here in Libya. As unappealing as it was to shepherd a unit of Italians around the desert, it was far preferable to being sent into the endless depths of Russia to wage a campaign that, as far as Steiner was concerned, was

195

pure madness. Out here in the desert, he had a degree of autonomy, of freedom that few other *Wehrmacht* commands provided.

Along with that autonomy, Steiner also believed that he had the power to decide when a situation was hopeless, and act in the best interests of his command. The ancient fort they occupied might have been formidable once upon a time, but in 1941, it was nothing but a gunnery exercise for an artillery officer and his battery. A couple of British "six-pounders" could knock the fortress into rubble within minutes, and far outrange anything he had at his disposal. If that artillery was defended by a couple of light anti-tank guns and some seasoned infantry, there'd be no way for him to counterattack without losing his entire command.

Steiner smiled grimly to himself, remembering how impressed Lieutenant Lewis had been when shown the outpost's defenses. Machine guns, mortars, anti-tank guns...all of them impressive to a man who commanded little more than a town car with a bit of armour plate and an oversized hunting rifle. But a squadron of Matilda tanks could roll right up to the base of his fortress with little difficulty while pounding his defenses to bits with their 40mm cannons and machine guns.

No, his greatest defense was being unnoticed out here in the desert. And now that the British knew where he was, even if he repulsed an attack by these Commandos, it would be just a matter of time before shells or bombs knocked his position into rubble. And when that happened, Steiner, the rest of his Brandenburgers, and the Italians would end up as nothing more than shriveled corpses buried in the sand, lost and forgotten by those who'd sent them here, another short list of names to be added to the miles-long butcher's bill.

Sorry, mein Führer, that's not going to happen.

Steiner let his field glasses hang around his neck and picked up his rifle before leaving the wall and descending down into the courtyard. He nodded to his senior non-com, Bauer, who was in the process of making his rounds, checking on all the weapon emplacements and ensuring none of the men were asleep or otherwise shirking their duties. Bauer saluted and walked over to Steiner.

"Sir, the *Bersaglieri* are awake and watchful. They are all well aware the enemy is out there tonight."

Steiner nodded. "Good. They're a dependable lot - for a bunch of foreigners. And our men are standing watch as well?"

"Four-man shifts every three hours, as you ordered, sir."

"Excellent," Steiner hesitated for a moment. "Arno, I want you to relay an order to the men, but only the Brandenburgers."

"Yes, sir?"

Steiner glanced around to make sure none of the Italians were within earshot. "I have every confidence in our men and the *Bersaglieri*, but if the unthinkable happens, and the situation here becomes hopeless, I do not want men risking themselves without cause."

Bauer looked rather perplexed. "Sir, I'm not sure I understand."

"What I'm saying, *Feldwebel*," Steiner whispered, "is that no German should die here if retreat is a viable option. Yes, stand and fight if we have hope of victory, but if we face only death or capture, it is for the good of the Reich that we go on to live and fight another day."

In the moonlight, Steiner saw Bauer's lips draw together in a thin line, a sign of displeasure he'd become all too familiar with over the last year. Bauer was an exceptional soldier, and a good sergeant as well, but he was of the 'do or die' school of soldiering, an unblinking adherent to the sorts of military ideals that had sent untold thousands of men marching into the meat grinders of the last war for little gain or purpose.

But in the end, Bauer was a soldier who followed orders. He snapped a textbook salute. "*Jawohl, Hauptmann.*"

Steiner returned the salute, then watched Bauer walk away before turning towards the barracks. It was time to attempt a few hours of sleep, and hope against hope they all lived through the night.

TWENTY-TWO

The Outpost
November 1st, 0030 Hours

The blade of Lynch's F-S knife punched deep into the small of the Italian's back, and the man's body arched against him, arms flailing, legs spasming. Lynch's other hand was clamped against the sentry's mouth, and his fingers gripped hard, digging into the soft flesh of the man's cheeks, spittle trickling through his fingers. Lynch drew the knife free and thrust again, this time bringing the blade around the body and up under the sternum, driving it deep into the heart. Through the knife's hilt, Lynch could actually feel the dying man's heart beat as it struggled, impaled on several inches of cold steel.

Finally, with a last shudder and the acrid stink of warm urine, the sentry died, and Lynch lowered him to the ground. Looking to his right, he saw Herring do the same to the sentry's partner. This pair had been patrolling the base of the hill, the last obstacle before the Commandos began their ascent up the western slope of the crescent. Price hadn't expected this side to be unguarded; the Germans were far too clever for that. But if approaching from an unexpected angle gave them even the slightest edge, Price and the rest of the squad were more than willing to give it a go.

Looking up the hill, Lynch cleaned and sheathed his knife, then turned as Price leaned in close.

"Take Herring up the hill with you. Find the path. Once you're there, give us three tugs on the line and we'll follow up. Then we make for the fortress, fast and hard as we can," Price whispered.

Lynch tapped Herring on the shoulder and the man nodded. Herring had one end of a heavy climbing rope looped across his torso, the line coiling over his shoulder and behind him to a pile on the ground. Both men slung their Thompsons across their backs, cinching the slings tight so the heavy, ten-pound weapons wouldn't slide around their bodies and bang against a rock. They also unbuttoned their pistol holsters, and by touch alone, both men confirmed their weapons were cocked, with a round in the chamber.

Not the safest way to carry a pistol whilst climbing up an unfamiliar hill in the dead of night, Lynch mused, *but to be sure, there isn't anything safe about this venture to begin with.*

Slowly, *very* slowly, the two Commandos began to scale the side of the hill. The angle was steep, and there was plenty of sand and grit covering every nook and handhold, which made finding a solid grip treacherous. Not for the first time, Lynch was grateful for their Commando-issue boots, which had soft rubber soles, well-suited for this sort of work without making much noise. The problem was ensuring no pebbles or flakes of rock were knocked loose and sent tumbling and rattling down the side of the hill, a feat made all the more difficult because the only way to find such loose debris was to make contact with it in the dark. On more than one occasion, Lynch and Herring both cringed at the seeming racket caused by a small stone skipping and bouncing down to the ground below, and the two men tensed, dreading the shouts and rattle of automatic weapons fire signalling their demise.

But the alarm was never raised, and after perhaps fifteen minutes, the two men made it to the top of the ridge. Crouching low and unslinging his Thompson, Lynch saw they were halfway along one "arm" of the crescent-shaped hill, about a hundred yards from the fortress itself. He saw the building's outline against the starry sky, but didn't see any sentries along the rooftop, nor did he see any movement anywhere along the ridge. There did appear to be a *sangar* halfway between them and the fortress, but no one inside noticed their presence.

Looking down the almost-vertical eastern slope, Lynch saw the dim outlines of covered shapes, probably vehicles shrouded with camouflage netting. Of particular interest was a large rectangle of netting almost directly below him. From where he crouched, Lynch noticed a pair of sentries walking a slow perimeter patrol around the netting, and he wondered if that was where the British prisoners were confined. There was going to be a lot of hot lead and steel flying through the air very shortly; he just hoped whoever was down there had the presence of mind to hit the dirt and stay down until the shooting stopped.

As Lynch kept watch, Herring made fast the climbing rope. Unable to use a hammer or stake to secure the line, they instead used a monkey's fist knot, with a thick wooden toggle through the middle. Herring found a suitable crack in the stone along the ridge, and with considerable effort, wedged the knot deep into the crack, making sure the wooden toggle was set so that weight from below would help keep the knot in place. The job completed, Herring gave the line three sharp tugs, and received two tugs in return. Feeling the rope go taut and satisfied after a few seconds that it would stay secured, Herring unslung his own weapon and took up a position back-to-back with Lynch.

Three men made it to the top of the ridge before their luck ran out. Lynch saw a figure begin a quick ascent along the ridge's footpath, running in his direction. The man moved with surprising speed along the ridge in the dark, and he wasn't going to give them anywhere near enough time before the rest of the squad made it onto the ridge. Lynch tapped the nearest man - it was McTeague - on the shoulder to draw the Scot's attention to the problem at hand. McTeague touched Lynch on the throat and drew his finger across in an obvious gesture. Lynch slung his Thompson over his shoulder so the weapon's distinctive outline was hidden from view and pulled his F-S knife free from its sheath. Rising from his crouch, he began to amble with a nonchalant gait down the ridge towards the approaching figure.

About fifteen feet away, the man noticed Lynch approaching and halted, muttering something in Italian that Lynch didn't understand. Needing a few more seconds, he simply grunted and muttered, "*Ja, ja,*" to the Italian.

The man gave him a strange look and said, "*Che cosa?*"

Lynch's free hand shot out and grabbed the Italian by the throat a split second before his knife rammed itself to the hilt in the man's chest. With surprising strength, the *Bersaglieri* lashed out, and he tore Lynch's hand away from his throat while stepping back, instinctively trying to pull himself free of the blade impaling his heart. Lynch lost his grip on the hilt of his knife and went after the man with a lunge, but his toe caught on a wrinkle of stone and he fell forward, his shoulder catching the man in the thigh.

With an inarticulate cry, the Italian fell off the ridge and plummeted down the side of the eastern slope, taking Lynch's knife with him. The Italian's body cartwheeled as it repeatedly smashed and slid along the rock face, finally coming to a stop in a mangled, boneless heap about ten feet from a horrified sentry. Lynch watched on his hands and knees, peering over the edge of the ridge, momentarily stunned at how completely and utterly he'd bolloxed the mission.

TWENTY-THREE

The Outpost
November 1st, 0055 Hours

With about five seconds before the sentry down below found the knife buried in the dead man's heart, Lynch decided that if they were in for a penny, they were in for a pound. He ripped a grenade from his web gear, pulled the pin, and threw it as hard as he could in the direction of what he assumed was the enemy's motor pool. Before the first grenade even hit the ground, it was followed by another. The first grenade exploded with a flat *crack*, shockingly loud in the silent desert night, and by the time the second grenade detonated, Lynch had already thrown his third.

A heartbeat after the third grenade exploded, the desert night lit up with fire. Lynch's first grenade must have punctured a vehicle's petrol tank, because the third grenade ignited a spreading pool of fuel, and in seconds, the flames reached the tank itself. With a *whooomp*, a ball of fire several yards in diameter rolled up into the sky, illuminating the crescent shape of the hill and the eastern face of the fortress.

Lynch was already running by the time his third grenade exploded. He charged back up the ridge, his Thompson in his hands, loudly whispering, "Don't shoot you bloody idiots, it's me!"

He skidded to a halt next to McTeague, whose shocked features were illuminated by the flames licking up into the air. The Scotsman grabbed Lynch and pulled him to within an inch of his face.

"Ye daft shite! What'd ye do that for?" he growled at Lynch.

"The bugger went over the edge, so he did!" Lynch gasped. "He still has my bloody knife sticking out of him. We've been rumbled for sure, so I threw a few eggs to make 'em look the other way."

"Oh, I do believe they're looking, all right," Lynch heard Price remark in the Englishman's usual dry tone.

Turning to look, he could see Italians and Germans running about below, some rushing towards the source of the flames with buckets of sand, others running away, wary of another vehicle explosion. Other men began firing randomly into the night, streams of machine gun tracers arcing into the darkness, ricocheting and careening off of rocks and tumbling through sand hundreds of yards away.

"How many men are up?" Lynch asked McTeague.

"Bowen, Johnson, and Nelson are still below," the sergeant replied.

Just then, there was a shout from the *sangar* between them and the fortress. A rifle cracked, and automatic weapons fire blazed at them from a pair of Italian machine pistols. Bullets smashed and ricocheted off of the stones around the ridgeline where they stood, and Stilwell grunted, dropping to one knee.

"Bloody hell!" he cried out. "Caught one in me thigh!"

"*Return fire!*" McTeague roared. "*Take that bloody position!*"

The squad put its enhanced firepower to good use. Dragging a limping Stilwell with him, McTeague advanced and fired the Bren one-handed, the buttstock tucked under his arm, the massive weapon rising with the heavy recoil doing some of the work for him. Higgins and Brooks steadied the muzzles of their slung Breda machine guns and cut loose with long bursts, stitching the stones of the *sangar* with fist-sized craters. One of the Italians was hit, and with a cry of agony, he stumbled away clutching his gut, then pitched headlong over the western edge of the ridge.

Lynch, Price, and several other Commandos added the firepower of their Thompsons, raking the *sangar* with short, chopping bursts of slugs. They advanced behind their suppressing fire, and finally took the position with a buttstroke to the face of the last surviving defender. The *sangar* was an anti-aircraft position, and contained a 20mm Breda cannon, similar to the weapon mounted inside the Autoblinda armoured cars. A crate containing twelve-round clips of 20mm cannon shells sat next to the Breda's mount, open and ready for action.

Behind them, first Nelson, then Bowen, and finally Johnson made it to the top, and as each man found his feet, he helped the other up and onto the ridge. With the entire squad together at last, the unit gathered at the captured *sangar* as Price issued his orders.

"Sergeant, take three men and begin sweeping down this side of the hill, clearing the enemy positions. Bowen, you and Johnson hold this *sangar* with Stilwell and begin the second phase of the assault. The rest of you lads are sticking with me - we're going to clear the fort."

"She looks buttoned up pretty tight, sir," Nelson said. "Want me to blow the door with a charge?"

"No, Corporal. I've got a better idea," Price replied. Smiling, he reached out and patted a hand against the Breda cannon's receiver.

Nelson's eyes went wide. "Oh...that's bloody brilliant! Can I?"

"Only if Sergeant McTeague doesn't need you. Dougal?" Price asked.

"I'm taking Higgins, Brooks, and Herring. Ye can have the rogue, Lieutenant. All right ye scallywags, on me. Stilwell, give Herring that bag of Eyetie magazines!"

Price's decision wasn't a moment too soon. As McTeague and the three other Commandos took off down the ridge towards the hill's southern weapons emplacements, the southern door to the fortress swung open, and a squad of *Bersaglieri* emerged. The men shouted in Italian towards the *sangar*, but seeing the four armed men moving away, and a number of other men clustered around the 20mm cannon, they quickly realized what all the recent gunfire was about. Rifles and machine pistols sent dozens of bullets towards Price and his remaining men, who now endured the same kind of withering fire they themselves had employed against the emplacement a minute ago. Slugs chipped stone and whined away, more than a few glancing off the steel mechanisms of the Breda cannon.

Price and the seven other Commandos flattened themselves against the ground, unable to even return fire against the Italians. Finally, Nelson pulled a Mills bomb from his webbing, and risking exposure, crouched and hurled the deadly missile towards the approaching enemy. The incoming fire slackened as the *Bersaglieri* scattered, and two more men threw grenades.

"Suppressing fire!" Price ordered. "Nelson, on that cannon! White, load him!"

The men sprang into action. As the rest of the Commandos pinned down the Italians, White slapped a clip of 20mm cannon shells into the Breda's receiver and Nelson sat in the gunner's seat, frantically spinning the elevation and traversing wheels. The cannon's barrel tipped down and swung to the left, pointing towards the fortress.

"Cover your ears lads!" Nelson shouted. "It's about to get loud!"

The Italians were just getting to their feet and bringing their weapons to bear when the slaughter began. The Breda opened fire with an immense roar, a six-foot tongue of flame leaping from its muzzle. As Nelson spun the traversing wheel and swept cannon fire across the enemy squad, men struck by the 20mm high-explosive shells were instantly destroyed, their bodies pulped, limbs shredded. One soldier had his head vaporized in the blink of an eye, his body toppling like a tree felled by a woodcutter. Another man was blown clean in half by a cannon shell in the belly, while the man next to him had his rib cage blown wide open, fragments of gleaming white bone spinning through the air.

The cannon fell silent. White slapped home another twelve-round clip, and Nelson swept the muzzle back across the enemy, further depressing the barrel's angle since anyone still alive was now pressed flat against the rocky ground. Bodies already ripped apart were further reduced to little more than rags and pulped meat, and after the second pass those few men still alive threw away their weapons and raised their hands into the air, pleading for their lives to be spared the horror of the cannon's wrath.

At this point, the entire garrison knew the enemy was among them. Rifle shots and bursts of machine pistol slugs came at the Commandos from all directions, but the *sangar* wall and the steep hill meant few of the defenders had a good firing angle. Furthermore, the guttering flames at the base of the hill created a host of flickering shadows that confused the defenders, causing many to fire on nothing but smoke and darkness.

The fortress was now shrouded in a cloud of rock dust knocked loose by cannon shells tearing holes in the wall big enough to stick a man's arm straight through. The heavy wooden door was gone, blasted to kindling by several cannon shells, and inside there were shouts and cries from wounded men.

"Sir?" Nelson asked, as White reloaded the cannon with another twelve rounds of high-explosive death.

Price peered through the dust and gloom at the men pleading on the ground, and the shattered stone wall of the fort, fifty yards away. "Corporal Nelson, tear that building apart. Corporal Bowen, it's your turn."

Bowen nodded, and pulled a wide-muzzled flare pistol from his pocket.

TWENTY-FOUR

The Outpost
November 1st, 0105 Hours

Sergeant McTeague advanced down the path, following the top of the ridgeline down the southern arm of the hill. His Bren was fully loaded and the two men on either side of him, Higgins and Brooks, carried their slung Breda machine guns at the ready. Behind the trio, Herring kept watch to their rear and flanks with a Thompson in his hands, the heavy bag of Breda magazines slung over his shoulder.

A short distance ahead of them, a *sangar* covered with camouflage netting concealed the low, menacing shape of a cannon. McTeague could hear several Italians talking in fevered tones, no doubt peering out into the moonlit desert, searching for the attackers causing all the havoc. From further up the hill came the slow, methodical hammering of the 20mm cannon, and the nearby Italians shouted and began traversing their gun, trying to bring it about so they could engage the cannon chewing their fortress into rubble.

"Easy now lads," McTeague growled. "Short bursts."

The three light machine guns ripped into the stone redoubt. Unprepared and exposed, the four men inside the *sangar* perished in a heartbeat, riddled with a dozen bullets. With little more than a few wet gurgles, the Italians sprawled and died where they stood, never knowing what killed them.

It took a few seconds' work to drag the bodies clear of the emplacement. A hundred yards further down the ridge, the three men manning a machine gun nest had seen the fate of their comrades, and brought their machine gun around to fire back up the ridge. They sent a blizzard of lead tearing into the anti-tank gun emplacement, forcing McTeague and the others to drop down onto their bellies as bullets smacked into stone and rang off the gun's armour shield.

"Prickly buggers, aren't they?" Herring shouted over the din as he dove for cover.

"Ach, load the bloody cannon!" McTeague shouted back, crawling on his hands and knees to the anti-tank gun's firing mechanism.

Herring opened a crate and pulled free a heavy 28mm armour-piercing shell, then rammed the shell home. As the breech locked itself, he leaned out of the gun's recoil path and grabbed another shell. McTeague took a deep breath, then raised himself up so he could peer through the gun-sight. The machine gun nest was lit up again by another burst of automatic fire, and ignoring the murderous hail rattling off rocks and steel plate inches from his face, the Scot centered the crosshairs on where he'd seen the muzzle blast, then tripped the firing mechanism.

The 28mm high-velocity cannon slammed back on its mount with a roar, flame spurting from its muzzle and dust swirling about from the blast. Herring immediately reloaded the weapon, and not bothering to fix his aim, McTeague fired again. There was the sound of ringing metal and a wavering cry of pain as the armour-piercing "squeeze bore" round smashed home at over four thousand feet a second.

"Another one, laddie!" McTeague ordered.

Herring loaded another shell, and McTeague fired again. This time the round sounded like it struck the *sangar* itself, with a crack of splintering stone. With a look of grim determination, McTeague fired one more shell into the machine gun nest, hearing the round pulverize steel and stone with its impact.

After the last shot crashed home, the four men sat in silence for a few seconds. There was no return fire from the machine gun, and each man privately shuddered at the thought of what such a terrible cannon could do to a man's body.

"Well, Sergeant?" Herring asked after a few seconds. "Do we clear that position?"

"Clear it?" McTeague replied. "I cannae think there's anything left."

Just then, a wavering red glow illuminated everything around them, and the men looked out to the north, towards the other arm of the crescent. A parachute flare burned crimson a hundred yards above the ridge, slowly sparking and smoking as it descended, bathing everything for several hundred yards in a flickering glow.

"Here it comes," McTeague said softly. "Poor buggers."

A moment later, the *whump* of a discharging three-inch mortar was heard from out in the desert. Seconds passed, and then an explosion blossomed in the night as a mortar bomb landed beneath the flare, several yards from a *sangar* housing a 20mm Breda anti-aircraft gun. A few seconds later more reports were heard in quick succession as the mortar crew fired for effect. Several of the ten-pound mortar bombs landed on target, pulverizing rock and shredding the Italians cowering inside their ineffectual defenses.

Brooks stood up to get a better look at where the mortar rounds were landing. "Bloody hell, looks like those Eyeties are really getting-"

As if he'd swallowed a live grenade, Brooks' body exploded in a shower of bloody meat and tattered rags. A split-second later, the boom of an anti-tank gun reached them from the other arm of the crescent.

Higgins wiped a sheen of blood and flesh from his face with his uniform sleeve. "What the blazes…?"

"Bloody Eyeties are givin' us a dose of our own medicine! Alright lads, let's shift this gun. Put yer backs into it!" McTeague ordered.

The three men shifted the gun mount, straining to move several hundred pounds of steel. They grabbed the split rail and dragged the gun back and around so that, with effort, it could be traversed to fire towards the other arm of the hill. Another anti-tank round clipped the top of the *sangar*, lacerating everyone with tiny, razor-edged stone splinters.

"They're getting closer!" Herring shouted.

McTeague lined up his shot, and as Herring loaded another round, the Scot fired at the distant target. Illuminated by the flare dropping out of the sky, the effect of the high-velocity anti-tank shell was easy to see. The round struck the stones making up the *sangar* and knocked several spinning through the air, one of them flying up to tear away the camouflage netting over the emplacement. At the same moment, the Italians fired again, and the three men felt the air buffet them as the projectile cracked past inches above their heads.

McTeague's second shot came in slightly higher, and the four Commandos saw sparks fly as the round tore through the 28mm anti-tank gun like it was a child's toy. Tiny, ant-like figures limped away from the emplacement, only to be picked off one at a time by single rifle shots.

"Sounds like Rhys is putting his lady to work," Higgins said.

"At that range, he cannae miss," McTeague replied.

"Well, Sergeant?" Herring asked. "What're we to do now?"

McTeague thumped the cannon with his fist. "Lads, let's find us another target."

TWENTY-FIVE

The Outpost
November 1st, 0110 Hours

With a disappointed sigh, Nelson fired the last of the 20mm cannon shells into the side of the fortress. He'd been having the time of his life, and was only sorry that after the first squad of Italians, no one had shown themselves to offer him a more exciting target. Nearly a hundred rounds of 20mm ammunition had been fired into the side of the stone fort. The wall appeared as if it was on the verge of collapse, in some places the holes large enough for a man to crawl through with ease.

"Alright lads, Nelson's had his fun. On your feet - we're clearing that building!"

Everyone except Bowen, Johnson, and Stilwell moved forward at a crouch, their Thompsons at the ready. Several times, one man or another slipped or skidded across glistening smears of human remains, and they struggled to avoid being sick in front of each other, gagging from the overwhelming slaughterhouse smell rising up from the horror at their feet. The three Italians who'd survived the barrage remained prone in the blood and gore, splattered in

220

so much human wreckage that they could have passed for dead men themselves. Lynch approached one Italian who looked up at him, tears cutting streaks in the dust and blood across the man's face. The once-proud soldier was now reduced to a weeping, trembling child.

"Sorry mate," Lynch muttered to the Italian. "Nothing personal."

The five men approached the shattered doorway, and at Price's signal, White lobbed a grenade into the courtyard beyond. The instant after the explosion, the five Commandos flowed through the entrance, Thompsons up and at the ready. The courtyard appeared empty save for a pair of corpses in the now-familiar uniform of the *Bersaglieri*, but immediately shots rang out, bullets smacking into the stone walls behind them. Lynch felt a bullet tug at his trouser leg, and the Commandos dove towards the nearest cover while spraying slugs at the muzzle flashes.

"Looks like I didn't get 'em all!" Nelson shouted above the din.

"It bloody well appears that way, doesn't it?" White shouted back.

Once they took stock of the situation, it was apparent there were only three or four riflemen on the other side of the courtyard. Not wanting to be pinned down here, Lynch and Nelson provided cover fire while the others moved towards the nearest building entrance. In a few seconds the five Commandos were inside the fortress proper.

"That was a hot reception!" quipped Hall.

Price shot him a silencing look. "Alright lads, we're going to do this one room at a time and make sure we've flushed out every last Jerry or Eyetie. Oh, and be sure we don't shoot any of those poor bloody prisoners, either."

While the momentum of the battle at large might have shifted in favor of the British, the Germans and Italians were far from beaten. Two rooms into their sweep, in a long, narrow mess hall, the Italians had set up a barricade of wooden tables and supply crates across a narrow doorway. Rifles and Beretta machine pistols cracked and chattered, sending slugs ricocheting off walls and around corners. Lynch felt a bullet fragment cut a stinging furrow across his ribs, and Nelson received a deep, bloody groove down the length of his forearm from a ricochet. Determined to break the stalemate, Price reloaded his Thompson, then dove out and rolled into the open, below the Italian's fire. With a sweep of his Thompson, Price ripped twenty .45 calibre slugs into the wooden table blockading the door, sawing a jagged tear across the barrier at waist-level. The shooting stopped abruptly, and seizing the initiative, the other Commandos ran past, their Thompsons roaring.

The barrier came apart under their withering fire, and the men smashed through, only to shout in alarm as fixed bayonets and rifle butts came at them from several angles at once. Lynch stumbled back, reeling from a glancing blow to the head from a buttstock, and brought his Thompson up just in time to deflect another blow strong enough to shatter a man's head like a melon. Lynch kicked out and heard his assailant curse in pain as he made contact with the man's groin. With a moment of freedom to act, Lynch drew his already-cocked .45 automatic from its holster. Firing from the hip, he put three bullets in his attacker's chest. The German, the same sergeant who'd accompanied Steiner to their meeting, gurgled out a curse as he stumbled back, clutching the ruin of his chest as he spun around and fell face-first to the floor.

Turning, Lynch saw the other Commandos were all on their feet, although several had acquired new cuts and bruises. Nelson wiped the blade of his trench knife across the tunic of the nearest Italian corpse, while rivulets of blood leaked down from his scalp. Hall fingered a nasty-looking notch carved out of his Thompson's buttstock.

"Closest I ever want to get to the tip of an Eyetie bayonet," he muttered.

Price gently massaged a battered jaw and holstered his smoking pistol while eyeing the dead man at his feet.

"Plucky lot, these *Bersaglieri.* That fellow loosened a couple of my back teeth with his last swing."

After everyone took a moment to steady themselves, the Commandos moved ahead swiftly, keeping an eye out not only for any lurking enemies, but any sign of the captured British soldiers as well. However, it soon became apparent they were flushing the last of the fort's defenders ahead of them. Pot-shots were taken in their direction from around corners and through doorways, forcing them behind cover and halting their pursuit. But, as soon as the Commandos returned fire and advanced, the resistance vanished.

As Lynch rounded a corner, a German stick-grenade flew towards him and on instinct he slapped it into an adjacent room with the butt of his Thompson. As everyone dove for cover, Lynch found himself on the floor, his head sticking out around the corner of the wall. Just as the grenade detonated he saw several men in German uniforms duck around a far corner moving at a run.

"Jerry's legging it, boyos!" he shouted.

"We've got 'em on the bloody ropes!" Nelson agreed. Every man took a second to load fresh magazines into their weapons, then they rose to their feet and hurried after their quarry.

Seconds later, the Commandos found themselves on the other side of the courtyard from where they'd entered. To their left, the northern doorway leading out of the fortress stood partially open. Crouching, Hall glanced outside, only to yank his head back a split second before several rifle bullets smashed holes in the wooden door.

"They're holding fast in another *sangar* about fifty yards away," he said. "Didn't look like a cannon though, maybe a mortar emplacement. Must be a dozen or more out there, Jerries and Eyeties."

Lynch looked at Price. "We go through that door now, and you can be sure they're going to blast us the same way we blasted them."

"Oh, I expect they're positively giddy at the thought," Price replied. "Any suggestions?"

"Well, if we can't go out," Nelson answered, "we might as well go up!" He pointed towards a set of stone stairs leading to the walkway around the courtyard wall, several yards above their heads.

"Good show! Alright lads, up we go," Price ordered.

The five men charged up the stairs and onto the walkway, taking care to stay low and out of sight. Each man found a place along the crenellations, and at Price's command, they peered over the edge of the wall and cut loose with their Thompsons.

At fifty yards away and firing in the dark, the Thompsons weren't ideal for the situation at hand. However, the amount of lead they put in the air more than made up for the range and poor visibility. Several cries of pain were heard from the *sangar*, but almost immediately, the Italians returned fire. Bullets snapped through the air around the Commandos' heads and punched craters into the stone battlements. A Beretta machine pistol chattered, and Lynch ducked as slugs ricocheted over his head and whined into the night.

"Lieutenant, this isn't working exactly as planned!" White shouted while reloading.

"Keep them guessing," Price ordered. "Fire and displace. Use the whole wall!"

The Commandos exchanged gunfire with the Italians for several minutes. Each man cut loose with a burst of slugs and ducked below the wall before moving to another firing position as return fire lashed at where they'd just been. Despite their best efforts, it didn't seem as if the Italians were taking any casualties. If they were losing men, those who remained were doing their best to make up for the losses.

As Lynch raised his head up over the edge of the wall again, he saw another flare slowly descending, this time over what remained of the enemy's motor pool. A few seconds

226

later, there came the slow, methodical *thumpthumpthump* sound of an autocannon out in the darkness, and he could see the flickering tongue of a muzzle flash, several hundred yards away. It was their captured Autoblinda, firing as it approached from the east. A moment passed, and then armour-piercing shells began to smash into the vehicles down below, tearing clean through the thin-skinned Bedfords parked neatly side-by-side under their camouflage netting.

Mortar bombs soon followed the cannon fire, exploding among the vehicles every four or five seconds. Although Eldred's Commandos had only brought one three-inch mortar with them, and a limited number of the ten-pound mortar bombs, the three men from Peabody's squad crewing the weapon were clearly experts in its use, bringing their shots down onto the targets designated by Bowen's flares with impressive accuracy.

One extremely well-placed mortar bomb struck the captured petrol tanker, and the immense blast sent a ball of fire rolling up into the sky, past the top of the fortress, and Lynch ducked as he felt the heat coming from the explosion over a hundred yards away. The entire outpost was lit up by the blast, and off to the east he could see the armoured cars and Desert Group vehicles approaching with crouching Commandos interspersed between them.

As the rolling ball of flame slowly dissipated, Lynch turned to the other Commandos, a wide-eyed look on his face. "I hope the poor bastards Jerry had in the bag weren't anywhere near *that!*"

The explosion had another immediate effect. Shouts of dismay came from the Italians in the *sangar*, and first one, then several other *Bersaglieri* threw their weapons over the edge of the emplacement.

"*Non sparare!*" they began to shout, and several hesitantly raised their hands in the air, surrendering.

Lynch looked over at Price. "Well, what do we do, now?"

Price frowned at the question. "I think the answer is quite obvious," he replied. "We accept their surrender. It's the only civilized thing to do."

TWENTY-SIX

The Outpost
November 1st, 0125 Hours

Lieutenant James Lewis had never been both so happy and so terrified at the same time in all his life. He and his fifteen men were face down in the dirt within their barbed wire enclosure, hands over their heads, as gunfire and explosions hammered the air all around them. Voices shouted nearby in Italian and German as boots pounded sand outside their fencing. Once, Lewis even thought he heard a few words of English, but with such a cacophony of noise he couldn't be sure.

One thing was certain, though. The outpost was being attacked, and it seemed from Lewis' vantage point - poor though it was - that his captors were losing. He could sense the uncertainty in their voices, the disorganized nature of their movements. In their minds, something was most definitely *not* going according to plan.

"*Freddy!*" Lewis whispered to the prone figure next to him.

"Aye, sir?"

"D'you see the little blighter?"

Lewis sensed Freddy shifting in the sand next to him.

"Aye, sir! He's off to my left. Hopping about like he's gotta take a piss. I think he's just too afraid of those Jerries to leg it."

"Is it just him? Do you see anyone else nearby?" Lewis asked.

Freddy shifted some more. "No, sir. It's just the one fellow, has himself one of those little Eyetie machine guns, sir."

"Do you have your rock, Freddy?"

"Aye sir, tucked in me pocket. Shall I spread the word?"

Lewis thought hard for a moment. "It's now or never, old bean. Soon as he's distracted and pointing that bloody perforator someplace else."

As much as he trusted Steiner - and that was probably as much as one could ever trust a German - Lewis understood his duty as an officer in the British armed forces. And that duty was to resist. Within a day of their capture, he'd instructed all of his men to find one or two well-shaped rocks, something sizable enough to use as a missile or a bludgeon, but small enough to hold and conceal easily. Over the course of a couple nights, each man dug about until they unearthed something of the proper size, at which point the makeshift weapon was surreptitiously tucked away in a place that was easy to remember, usually at a specific point underneath the prisoner's bedroll.

When the first three explosions shattered the silence of the night, Lewis thought there might have been an accident. But when gunfire followed shortly thereafter, quickly escalating into a full-fledged firefight, Lewis knew someone was attacking the base. The cannon fire up on the ridge confused him for a moment, and he wondered if the first explosions had been bombs, but he immediately dismissed the idea. He'd not heard any aircraft engines, and the bombs were far too small.

No, they were being infiltrated, possibly by men of the Desert Group, or maybe that newly-formed irregular raiding unit - Detachment "L" - that everyone was whispering about. Lewis guessed that those first three explosions had probably been some kind of distraction to sow confusion while the raiders launched their attack. At the start, he had been content to keep his men low and quiet, hopeful that someone would be along soon to shoot their gaoler and set them free. But now, as cannon fire, mortars, and anti-tank guns roared all around them, Lewis grew more worried they'd be on the receiving end of a poorly-aimed mortar bomb or grenade, and that'd be the end of it all.

Suddenly, there were a series of high-velocity impacts, as autocannon fire tore into the vehicles parked to the north of their tent. The sounds of tortured, ringing metal were quickly followed by several mortar bombs exploding amongst the motor pool, and in an instant, a massive conflagration lit up everything bright as day. Lewis felt the heat against his skin, and risked a look up from forcing his face into the sand. A few feet away, their guard was shakily picking himself up from the ground.

"Now, lads! Now!" Lewis shouted.

The men overcame their fear and jumped to their feet. The Italian, sensing movement behind him, turned just in time to receive a fast pitch to the side of the head from one of Lewis' men, the fist-sized rock smacking home with an audible *thud*. The guard staggered and made a motion to raise his Beretta machine pistol, but the first rock was followed by several more in quick succession, and one of them caught him square between the eyes. The guard lurched drunkenly, and with a mumbled curse, fell flat on his face, the gun tumbling from his hands.

"The fencepost!" Lewis shouted. "The corner post!"

Two of his strongest men ran to the corner post closest to the guard. Each man grabbed ahold of the fence post with both hands and put all their strength into bending it back towards them. The post, two inches in diameter, resisted for a few agonizing seconds, but with a sharp *crack*, snapped clean through just above the sand. The two men dropped the post, and as soon as the barbed wire fell safely to the ground, they were charging over the barrier.

The guard managed to raise his head off the ground just a moment before an Englishman's booted foot connected with his temple. The guard let out a groan and raised a pleading hand above his head, but before his attacker could get the boot in again, Lewis grabbed the man by the shoulder.

"That's enough lad. Get his gun and let's find some cover," Lewis ordered.

The rest of the men jumped over the downed wire, but once free from captivity, Lewis didn't know what to do. There were still shots ringing out in the darkness, and he saw a number of *Bersaglieri* rushing about, many heading towards the undamaged vehicles. Lewis motioned for the men to go prone, hopefully avoiding any stray bullets or shell fragments zipping through the air.

"Sir, look!" Freddy shouted next to Lewis, pointing into the moonlit desert beyond the firelight.

Lewis turned his head and saw three lumbering shapes - a pair of familiar Morris cars and a larger Autoblinda, its 8mm machine gun tearing long bursts at the Italians. The lumpy, irregular profiles of the overburdened Desert Group vehicles were right behind the armoured cars, their Lewis and Vickers guns spraying tracers towards the northern arm of the crescent hill, trading fire with the stubborn defenders. Scattered among the vehicles was a skirmish line of Commandos, weapons raised and firing on any target that presented itself.

As Lewis watched, an Italian machine gun raked a line of tracers across several Commandos and one of the Chevrolets. The men dropped like puppets with their strings cut, and the truck lurched to a halt and began to burn fiercely, its petrol tank ripped open by bullets, the tracers igniting the fuel as it spilled. In the firelight, Lewis didn't see anyone get up off the ground or climb out of the burning vehicle.

Off to his left, one of the Autoblindas began firing its 20mm cannon, hammering a stream of shells towards the attacking British. Several rounds hit one of the Morris cars, sparks flying as the armour failed to stop the heavy calibre shells. The Morris slewed back and forth for a moment before coming to a stop, the Boys rifle in its turret still firing every few seconds. Before the defenders' Autoblinda could fire another twelve-round clip from its autocannon, there was a terrible impact on the armoured car's front hull. A moment later, a loud report came from the east, out in the desert. When a second shot crashed home, tearing through the car's turret, Lewis guessed the weapon was a light anti-tank gun - no match for the Autoblinda, which now sat silent, the crew either dead, wounded, or cowering in terror.

But the fight wasn't over yet. The *Bersaglieri* were organizing, NCOs ordering their men into firing lines behind any available cover. Disciplined rifle fire began to pepper the British vehicles and the advancing Commandos, many of whom moved to place the armoured cars between them and the defender's rifle fire. The Italians seemed to rally, shouting insults at the British and encouragement to each other, but their elation was short-lived. The two mobile armoured cars and the LRDG trucks closed quickly, and more than a dozen machine guns ripped into the Italian lines, hundreds of bullets hammering into vehicles, supply crates, stone, sand, and flesh. With the *Bersaglieri* pinned down, the Commandos were able to move out from behind the armoured cars, and they quickly added their rifles, Thompsons, and Bren guns to the onslaught.

Vastly outgunned, outnumbered, and all too quickly surrounded, the defenders finally accepted their fate. Surviving NCOs blew whistles and shouted to their men, and the rifle fire ceased. The British gunfire quickly died out as well, and for the first time in what seemed to Lewis like hours, there was silence.

Lewis turned to Freddy with a broad grin across his face. "Looks like we'll finally get a proper cup of morning tea, old bean."

TWENTY-SEVEN

The Outpost
November 1st, 0600 Hours

As dawn rose over the captured outpost, the full scale of the battle was evident. The ground along the ridgeline to the south of the fort was a horror-show, even after the larger remnants of the Italian dead had been dragged to the side of the path and covered with bedrolls taken from the fortress' barracks. Some of the dead had to be shoveled out of the *sangars* hit by anti-tank shells or mortar bombs. Men killed by grenade blasts or gunfire seemed almost peaceful in comparison to those who'd been pulverized by the heavier weapons, but even those largely intact corpses were quickly gathering flies and other curious, hungry, crawling investigators.

Lynch bent over a crumpled body and slowly rolled the man over. The Italian's sightless eyes were covered in grains of sand, and flies were already exploring the corners of his mouth and nose. Reaching down, Lynch grasped the handle of his Fairbairn-Sykes knife and put his boot against the corpse's belly. With a heave, he dragged his weapon free, wiping the bloody blade clean with a corner of the dead man's jacket. The knife's hilt was tacky with dried blood, and the flies wouldn't leave it alone. Lynch slipped the blade back into its scabbard until he could clean it better, then rolled the corpse back into his original position, face towards the sheer rock wall of the hillside.

"Found it?" Nelson asked as he approached.

"Aye. A wee bit messy to be sure, but it'll clean up just fine," Lynch replied.

"That's good, you know they'd probably take it out of your bloody pay otherwise."

Lynch nodded absently, his gaze lifting from the body at his feet. His eyes swept across the rest of the destroyed outpost. Smoke still curled up into the morning sky from the burning vehicles, and further off he saw Donovan and Peabody leading their men as they policed the remaining enemy dead, collected weapons, searched pockets for any intelligence to give the officers or valuables to take as souvenirs.

Fifty feet away, Lynch saw Herring bending over a German corpse. With practiced movements, Herring frisked the body and took several items, including a Luger he tucked into the back of his waistband. As if sensing he was being watched, Herring turned and looked at Lynch, staring for a few seconds before he gave a mocking salute and moved on to another body.

"Bit of a queer one, ain't he?" Nelson remarked, also watching Herring go about his grisly business.

"Aye, so he is. I'm sure now we don't know of the half of it."

Lynch turned and began walking with Nelson towards the rest of their squad, gathered near the Italian prisoners. Along with Brooks, four of Eldred's Commandos and three New Zealanders had been killed in the final assault, with five other men wounded. Of the nearly fifty *Bersaglieri* who'd garrisoned the outpost, almost three dozen had been killed in the fighting. The remainder surrendered when the outcome of the battle was inevitable, half of them taken prisoner by Price's squad. Only one of the Germans was taken alive, knocked senseless by flying debris when the petrol tanker blew up. Four other Germans were killed, all while leading small bands of *Bersaglieri* like those who'd ambushed Lynch and the others inside the fortress.

Of *Hauptmann* Steiner and the remaining Germans, there was no sign. While rounding up the Italians, Lynch had found a knotted rope tied to a large steel pin driven into the stone at the edge of the western slope near the northwest corner of the fortress wall. He'd pointed it out to Price, who surmised that the Germans had used it as a last-ditch escape route, choosing to flee across miles of trackless desert rather than face death or capture. Where Steiner and his men were going, however, Lynch couldn't imagine.

"I can't tell you how good it is to have a properly prepared cup of char. Those Italians never could get it right."

Lynch turned, and saw the Hussars lieutenant standing behind him, holding two mugs of tea laden with sweetened milk. Lewis handed one to Lynch and the other to Nelson, who bobbed his head and offered a brief "Thank you, sir".

"Much appreciated, sir," Lynch said. "Glad to be of service. It couldn't have been easy sitting out here for days. I was in the bag once, meself. Wasn't a very pleasant experience."

Lewis nodded. "I hate to admit it, but although they were the enemy, they weren't a right pack of jackals, either. Steiner would have me up to the fortress for a nightcap most evenings, if you can believe it."

"I do, actually," Lynch replied. As Lewis walked away to join the other officers, Lynch looked over at the *Bersaglieri*, now confined in the same barbed wire fencing Lewis' men had occupied only hours ago. Most of the Italians looked ragged and bloody, and several of them were swaddled with field dressings. They all had the dazed, blasted look of men who hadn't yet come to terms with how quickly their situation had changed.

Fortune in war is a fickle thing, Lynch mused. He took a sip from his mug of tea.

It was perfect.

TWENTY-EIGHT

The Libyan Desert
November 1st, 0700 Hours

Hauptmann Karl Steiner pulled back the canvas tarpaulin and exposed the front bumper of a Kübelwagen. It'd taken half an hour of digging with rifle butts and bare hands to expose the front of the car, but as Steiner continued to pull away the protective cover he saw the cars appeared to be in good condition. Months ago, he'd tucked them close against the leeward side of a small, sheer-sided rock formation and covered them with camouflage netting and canvas dust covers. However, he hadn't predicted the cars being buried by a sand storm.

"Alright boys," he said. "Almost there. Grab shovels, and let's uncover the other two before we take a water break."

One of the remaining Brandenburgers unclipped a shovel from the side of the exposed Kübelwagen, and another man pulled a second tool from the passenger seat. Taking turns, the six men remaining in his command set about unburying all three cars.

Feldwebel Bauer had thought Steiner was being foolish and perhaps even a bit cowardly hiding "getaway cars" miles away from their base of operations. But Bauer wasn't here, he was back with the Italians, either dead or captured, and Steiner was defeated, but alive and free to fight another day. According to Steiner's worldview, that was all that mattered.

Finally, one of the cars was freed from enough sand that Steiner could climb into the driver's seat. He worked the starter, and after a couple of worrying sputters, the engine finally caught and steadied. He reached behind him and pulled a canteen out of a haversack, then unscrewed the top and took a long swig of tepid, metallic water. Looking over, he saw his men finish unearthing the other two vehicles. Steiner raised his canteen in a salute.

"*Macht schnell*, boys!" Steiner ordered. "We've got almost three hundred kilometers to drive, and I'm buying the first round!"

Author's Note

Some have called the North African campaign of World War Two "the last gentleman's war". I imagine that sentiment is cold comfort for the souls of all the dead men lying in forgotten graves scattered across the desert landscape. When compared to the brutal, merciless slaughter of the Normandy beach landings and the Falaise Pocket, the horrors of the Stalingrad and Leningrad sieges, or the wanton barbarity of the Red Army's advance into Germany, the North African battles might be considered almost civilized.

Almost.

The desert is a terrible place to make war. Scorching hot during the day and freezing cold at night, with little water and poor lines of resupply. No cover or concealment to speak of, except for whatever trenches or *sangars* you could fashion with your hands and an entrenching tool. Infantry would bake in the sun when they weren't being shelled or shot at, while tankers would bake in their rolling ovens when they weren't being torn to pieces by armour-piercing shells and hull fragments, or burning alive inside their own vehicles. I vividly recall reading one account of a tank battle in North Africa where a dismounted tanker watched in horror as liquefied fat from burning men dribbled through the burst seams of a shattered tank a few feet from his position. Gentlemen's war or no, burning to death trapped inside a tank is not a good way to die.

After barely surviving their mission in Calais, I decided it was time to even the odds a little for our heroes, making them a part of a larger, more formidable unit. It also gave me the chance to move the story from northern France, where very little was actually happening, to someplace where Britain was at the time holding its own against the Axis. North Africa was also the place where a lot of new irregular units – such as the Long Range Desert Group and the Special Air Service – were created. The lack of strong, defensible borders, the need for intelligence gathered far behind enemy lines, and the vulnerability of supply routes and depots made the desert battlefield the perfect place to incubate special operations tactics. The lessons learned during the battles for North Africa are still studied and applied by Special Forces here in the 21st century.

In conclusion, I want to thank those who took time out of their busy lives to read the rough draft of *Operation Cannibal* and provide feedback: Dan Eldredge, Mark Allen, Matthew Higgins, John Pritchard, Frank Moody, Sean McLachlan, and David Foster. I also want to thank the talented Ander Plana for *Operation Cannibal*'s cover. And, finally, I want to thank everyone who bought the previous novels in the COMMANDO series. Your support – past, present, and (hopefully) future - is *greatly* appreciated.

So, what is next for Lynch and his companions? Well, Operation Crusader takes place seventeen days after the end of this story, and a few dozen heavily-armed Commandos *might* come in handy…

Contact Me

My blog, Post Modern Pulp:
http://www.postmodernpulp.com

You can find me on Facebook:
https://www.facebook.com/jack.badelaire

You can also find me on Twitter: @jbadelaire

Printed in Great Britain
by Amazon